AT LAST IN LAGUNA

ROMANCE IN LAGUNA BEACH
BOOK TWO

CLAIRE MARTI

To everyone who believes they aren't worthy of love and to those who prove them wrong.

CHAPTER 1

Alyssa Morgan gripped her champagne flute in her left hand and curled the fingers of her right hand into a fist. How had she been recruited for the traditional wedding bouquet toss? The last place she wanted to be was among the pack of women vying to snag a bunch of flowers.

In fact, she'd hidden in the restroom, positive she could evade the single ladies' ordeal and drink her bubbly in peace. But her new sister-in-law, Sophie Morgan, née Barnes, refused to begin the archaic ritual without her. The other bridesmaids hunted her down and corralled her back to the dance floor.

Fine. So here she was, wedged into the middle of the group. She'd pretend to participate. Nothing short of a cattle prod to the back could induce her to catch the unwanted prize for herself.

While she was thrilled her brother, Nick, had found his happily ever after with Sophie, Alyssa doubted she'd be so lucky. After all, she'd fallen in love with her big brother's best friend, Brandt Michael Dempsey, the moment she'd set eyes on him when she was an awkward teenager.

Over the last decade, he'd failed to notice her, except as his buddy's baby sister.

Until the Christmas party. Or as she preferred to call it, "The Mistletoe Incident."

With a single embrace, he'd blown away every schoolgirl fantasy in which he'd starred. One kiss forever imprinted in her heart. One passionate, mind-blowing kiss had ruined her for anyone else.

Because she couldn't forget that desire warred with shock in his ocean-blue eyes when he'd lifted his mouth from hers. He'd wanted her, too. He'd bolted early from the annual party and avoided her ever since.

Brandt didn't date the same woman twice and had the dubious title of Player of Laguna. Her catching a wedding bouquet—superstition or not—wouldn't fix his commitment issues nor make him love her back. But her brother relinquished his title as the other Player of Laguna after meeting Sophie, so who knew?

An icy burst of liquid splashed her arm.

Her champagne spilled, thanks to a redhead jostling her in a desperate attempt to get closer to the bunch of white roses Sophie tossed.

"Mine, mine," the annoying woman screeched, flapping her arms like a goose attempting flight, and knocked Alyssa's glass to the ground.

She leaped out of the way to avoid ruining the elegant aquamarine silk dress she'd actually considered wearing again. Unlike the collection of hideous bridesmaid dresses stuffed into the back of her closet.

Something smacked into her chest. On reflex, both hands flew up and somehow she ended up clutching the flowers. Bemused, she gazed down at the snowy-white blooms secured in aqua and silver satin ribbon. Unable to resist, she sniffed the fragrant blossoms, inhaling their heady aroma. Just for a moment.

"That's mine." The ginger terror pounced and wrestled to filch the bouquet.

No longer willing to give up the flowers, she backed away from the frenzied creature. "Back off. Stealing a bouquet isn't going to help you find a husband. You already knocked my drink out of my hand."

When she glanced up, her new sister-in-law stared at her with a devious smirk.

Sophie had thrown it directly to her, the brat. Alyssa waved the flowers overhead in victory. Who was she to upset Sophie on her wedding night? She had played matchmaker for Nick and Sophie, and apparently, now the tables were turned.

Maybe it was a sign.

The hair on the back of her neck rose, and she turned and locked eyes with Brandt. In his best man's black tuxedo, he looked gorgeous, with his dark, wavy hair ruffled by the wind and his square-jawed face unsmiling.

For a moment, the clamor of the outdoor wedding reception receded, and she stood motionless in the heat of his piercing gaze. Oblivious to the hundred-plus revelers surrounding them, they stared at each other. His lips quirked up at the corners when his gaze dropped to the flowers clutched in her hands. Like a record starting up again, the music rushed back in, and the spell was broken.

Enough. This situation was ridiculous. She stalked through the crowd toward him. His expression was once again impassive despite her purposeful approach.

"You. Come here now." She caught his hand and tugged him toward a cluster of trees bordering the perimeter of The Ranch at Laguna Beach's dreamy romantic venue.

Away from the lights, laughter, and fancy cocktails.

Into the secluded shadows.

"What are you doing?" His voice was raspy.

Three glasses of champagne fueled her courage. When they reached a private spot, she whirled toward him and threw her arms around his strong tanned neck, pressing him up against a tree. Even when she sported four-inch stilettos, he still towered over her.

She'd had enough of loving him from afar. What did she have to lose?

"Alyssa…" He shifted away, but the enormous tree prevented him from going far.

She thrust her fingers into his thick hair, dragged his head down, and poured all her repressed passion into the kiss. For a moment, he remained immobile, unresponsive.

Oh no.

With a growl, he banded his arms around her and hauled her against his lean muscular frame. He deepened the kiss and stroked his tongue against hers. She melted against him, enveloped in his hot embrace. One large hand slid up and gripped a handful of her hair, holding her in place. His other hand stroked down her back, fisting in the thin silk of her gown, pressing her against every rock-hard inch of him.

A kaleidoscope of stars burst behind her eyes. Kissing him exceeded every sensation she'd ever experienced. Heat curled down her spine, and she arched closer.

"Brandt," she murmured when he broke the kiss.

He lowered his forehead against hers, his breath harsh, his heart pounding against hers. He couldn't deny he was just as affected by their kiss as she was. Tremors tingled along her skin, and she couldn't resist nibbling along his neck, inhaling his fresh, masculine scent.

She wanted more.

He sucked in a sharp breath and clasped her bare shoulders, creating unwelcome distance between them. "Alyssa."

"Don't push me away…please." Was that her voice? So breathless? So shaky? So desperate?

She couldn't discern the expression in his eyes in the twilight.

"We can't do this. I'm not the right guy for you." He looked away, back toward the wedding reception.

Her breath hitched. "Why? Because of Nick?"

"Among other things." He maneuvered away, widening the divide between them.

Without the heat from his body, a chill snaked across her skin. She shivered. "Nick's married now. He wants me to find happiness too."

"Exactly. You want it all. The white picket fence, the two point five. Sorry, babe, but that's not me." He shook his head, his lips pressed in a tight line.

"Not two point five kids. Try four or five, like enough for a football team." Squaring her shoulders, she injected confidence into her voice. "But don't worry. I'm not asking you to marry me. I have a proposition for you."

Because after that mind-blowing Christmas kiss, Brandt couldn't deny their physical chemistry was explosive. And his response tonight confirmed he was attracted to her. Maybe if they slept together and got each other out of their systems, she'd be able to move on.

Or she'd change his mind.

"A proposition?" One dark brow arched.

"I know you want me. You've stayed away because Nick acts like an overprotective father from the 1950s. Well, I'm not a child for him to take care of anymore. I'm twenty-nine."

When he remained silent, she stepped closer. Stroked one hand down his chest. This time he didn't back away. "Have a fling with me. No strings. Two weeks while Nick and Sophie are on their honeymoon. It will be our secret."

He had to agree. Didn't he?

He barked out a laugh. "You're out of your mind. How much champagne have you had?"

Her stomach clenched. "Brandt?"

"Come on, Alyssa. You aren't my type. Not even close." He raked his gaze over her head to toe. "You're like a little sister, not a hookup."

"But you kissed me back. You do want me." His earlier response wasn't fake and certainly hadn't been brotherly.

"I'm a guy." He shrugged, a cold mask slipping over his face. "You caught me off guard, but I just don't want you that way. Definitely not enough to risk my friendship with Nick."

Her throat tightened. "You're lying."

He turned away and shoved his hair away from his face. "Just stop, okay? You're embarrassing both of us."

"Why are you being such a jerk?" *Why are you breaking my heart?*

"This is me, babe. Now go pursue a nice guy."

"Go to hell and don't call me 'babe.'" She pivoted and stalked away, her spine rigid.

"Alyssa."

She stopped but refused to look at him. He crossed the grass, silent as a leopard stalking prey, but she sensed him when he reached her.

"You'll need this to catch yourself a husband." He thrust the bouquet into her hands.

Without turning, she gripped the flowers with one hand and flipped him off with the other. Jerk.

She marched directly to the bar and slammed a tequila shot. She waved off the saltshaker and slice of lime from the bartender. Flames erupted in her throat, and fire ignited in her belly. Gasping like a fish out of water, she doubled over, surreptitiously wiping the tears streaming down her cheeks. Well, hell, that warmed up the veritable bucket of ice Brandt had just tossed on her.

She slapped the glass back onto the bar. The last time she'd taken a shot of tequila had been back in college. Apparently, she wasn't equipped to handle it. Just as she hadn't been prepared for Brandt's chilly rejection. She dabbed her eyes with a monogrammed aqua cocktail napkin, offering a silent thank-you to the makeup artist who'd insisted she wear waterproof mascara.

"Tough night?" Her new sister-in-law's amused voice queried from her left.

"Yes, still recovering from that ginger wrestling me for the bouquet. Which I did *not* want, as you are well aware. What was that all about?" She swiveled and narrowed her eyes.

Sophie held up her hands. "I know you want to get married, and now that Nick can focus on his own love life instead of yours, maybe he won't scare off the next guy you date."

"Huh." Alyssa huffed and studied the flowers still clasped in her hand.

A twinge of guilt hit her. So, maybe she'd allowed everyone to believe Nick's gruff exterior caused the guys she dated to drop like flies after a few dates. Not that she'd been the one swatting them away because nobody could compare to Brandt. He represented the standard against which she'd measured other men, for better or for worse.

And tonight definitely felt like "worse."

"Hey, was that tequila? Are you okay?" Sophie asked, all hints of humor dissipating.

Sophie had no clue about Alyssa's unrequited feelings, and she certainly wasn't going to confess now. Brandt had made it abundantly clear he didn't want her. Despite his obvious arousal when he'd kissed her.

His harsh dismissal resurrected her old insecurities from high school when everyone made fun of her. All knobby knees and elbows. The braces and headgear. The hideously thick glasses that were unfortunately the only ones that enabled her to see past the tip of her own nose. The gawky ugly duckling. The tremendous need she'd felt for control…

"Alyssa?" Worry colored Sophie's voice and she brushed her forearm.

"I'm fine, I'm fine. Don't worry about it." *Convince yourself of that one, girl.* "How are you, Mrs. Morgan?" No way would she ruin Nick and Sophie's wedding night with drama.

"Mrs. Morgan. I love it." Sophie's face lit up. "I love your brother so much, and I'm so happy you're my sister now, not just my friend. Do you promise everything is okay? I hate to leave for France for two weeks if something's going on."

"Don't be silly. I'm great. I always am." After she and Nick had been orphaned, she'd honed her external demeanor and learned to tuck away emotions she didn't want to share. And wouldn't that skill come in handy tonight?

"Well, we'll check in from Antibes, and not just for status reports on how my kitty is doing. Are you excited to start working on Tearmann House?"

Tearmann House was the center for abused women and children Brandt founded as one of his latest philanthropic ventures. Nick was the architect, and she was the interior designer. Nick's initial portion was finished, and he'd handed the baton to her for the build-out and design.

Over a year ago or pre-Mistletoe Incident, the arrangements seemed simple. Create an interior to complement Nick's design and Brandt's vision. Everything from final decisions on walls and rooms down to color schemes, furniture, art, and even linens for the residential portions. She'd been accumulating cut sheets and concepts in her project binder for months.

Maybe she should have thought about that before she'd

blithely propositioned Brandt. How could she work with him now?

Her cheeks heated and she cleared her throat. "Um, I'm supposed to check in with the project manager on Monday. With all the zoning and permitting delays postponing the construction, my start date has changed several times. But I'm ready to go."

"I know Brandt's really excited to finally move forward. Nick said this center is deeply personal to him. Where is he anyway?" Sophie tilted her head.

"Brandt? I don't know where he is. Why would I know?" Alyssa jolted and whirled her head around, scanning the crowd. When she didn't see him, relief filled her.

Because right now she couldn't face him. No more tequila shots—liquor transformed into truth serum and no way was she sharing her rejection with anyone. Tonight was about celebrating true love. She'd lick her wounds in private for now, thank you very much. Later tonight she could wallow in a tub of mint chocolate chip ice cream after the bride and groom left the reception.

She forced herself to focus on the stunning setting. The dance floor shimmered like *A Midsummer's Night Dream*-type bower, surrounded by trees adorned with hanging tea lights. Subtle fragrance from vases of ivory and ice-blue flowers combined with the light ocean breeze. The glowing white canopy shrouded everything with a romantic glow. Maybe that's why she'd thrown caution to the wind?

Sophie's brilliant blue eyes narrowed, and Alyssa forced her lips to curve up. "We should be dancing."

"Yes, we should." Sophie grabbed her hand and dragged her onto the dance floor where the DJ was playing the awful wedding reception classic "We Are Family."

She loved weddings—usually. And she was over-the-moon thrilled for Nick and Sophie. She was. But after

Brandt's rejection, her deepest desire for a husband and sports team worth of children seemed as likely to happen as her flying to Mars. Unfortunately, not one of the hundreds of lights surrounding them appeared to be a spaceship. It figured.

Time to put on her big-girl panties.

Kelly, Sophie's striking best friend, and maid of honor, joined them on the dance floor. Digging deep, Alyssa threw her arms up in the air and shook her hips to the beat. She danced with Sophie, Kelly, and a few of the other brides-maids who'd joined them.

She'd lose herself in the music and wipe Brandt from her mind.

CHAPTER 2

*B*randt remained in the shadows and nursed his whiskey. And, yeah, watched Alyssa swaying on the dance floor. Success—he'd sent her running. The one other time they'd kissed, he'd been the one to flee. At a Christmas party last year, under the mistletoe, he'd laughed and leaned down to give his best friend's little sister a chaste peck.

And the moment their lips met; the earth stopped spinning on its axis. One kiss had rocked his world. Over the last year, he'd distanced himself from the social occasions he'd known she'd attend and tried like hell to make sure he was never alone with her. Because he kept his relationships casual for a reason.

Hell, he still remembered Alyssa from when he and Nick became friends over a decade earlier. She'd been a brainy, gangly teenager, her sparkling blue eyes not quite concealed behind thick coke-bottle glasses. She had stared at him with hero worship.

Unwarranted admiration. Even then, he'd known she'd grow into a stunning woman and her schoolgirl crush would disappear. Apparently, he'd miscalculated on the crush. Somehow, despite his lack of encouragement, she wanted him. Or more accurately, her romanticized version of whom she believed him to be.

And now, Alyssa propositioned him to a no-ties two-week fling? While his best friend, a.k.a. her insanely protective big brother and sole living relative, was out of town?

She'd lost her mind. She'd make him lose his. He shook his head, trying to remove the imprint of her body against his. Erase her intoxicating citrus scent that clung to his clothes.

She was too damned sexy, with her smoky blue eyes and her obvious desire for him. A vision of her long, lean limbs wrapped around him, her beautiful full lips swollen from his kisses, and her perfect skin flushed with passion jolted him again.

He pressed one hand against the sharp pain piercing his gut. No fucking way could he ever have her. He could never deserve her--never be the man she needed. She was the perfect woman. Sleeping with Alyssa would be the biggest mistake of his life. Both of their lives.

He'd done the right thing. Avoiding her was the only way he could protect her.

"Hiding out?"

His breath caught and turned to face his best friend. "Dude, you startled me. Just taking a little breather. You know weddings aren't my scene."

Nick's gaze was glued to his new wife on the dance floor. "Now that's an understatement." He chuckled.

"I'm happy for you. Sophie's great. You two are lucky." Brandt thumped him on the back.

"Thanks. It means a lot coming from you." Eyes wide, Nick turned toward him.

Brandt shrugged a shoulder. No need to get sappy. Nick

was his oldest, closest friend, but they had their guy code. And said code didn't include displays of sentiment.

"Hey, can you do me a favor?" Nick asked.

"Sure, anything." He took another sip of whiskey.

"Can you keep an eye on Alyssa for me while we're in Europe?"

Brandt sputtered. "What? Why?"

Nick grimaced. "You know, maybe just check in on her or something? She's been on those online dating sites, and there are a bunch of creeps on there. I want to make sure she's safe."

"Come on, she's twenty-nine years old. She doesn't need a babysitter, and I'm not the guy to do it anyway." Panic shot through his system.

If Nick discovered what his baby sister had just proposed…

He swallowed the guilt, remembering his instant arousal when she kissed him. The things he'd wanted to do with her. Still wanted to do. His bowtie choked him, suddenly a size too small.

He swallowed to alleviate the tightness in his throat.

Nick laughed. "Who better than a player to recognize another one, right? Seriously, I trust you. You're the closest thing to a brother we have, and she's always listened to you. Besides, you guys will be starting on the center next week, right? So you'll see her a lot."

Shit, he'd have to work with her. See her beautiful face. Listen to her melodic voice. But not touch her. How was he going to look at her on Monday morning without imagining the two of them together? Naked. He was screwed.

"Hey, you awake? Promise me you'll look out for her."

"Yeah, yeah, grandma. But she's not a kid anymore." If only Nick knew how true the statement was.

"You and Alyssa are the only family I've got besides

Sophie, and I won't have some scumbag taking advantage of her. She's been through too much already. Just act like a big brother."

Big brother? Would he stop with the sibling reference already? Maybe a decade ago.

"Of course. But if she finds out you asked me, she's going to kick your ass." Brandt nodded even as his stomach knotted into ropes.

"No shit. So don't tell her. Now come on, I need my best man back at the reception." Nick patted his shoulder. "I love you like a brother, man. I appreciate it."

Warmth filled Brandt's chest. Nick was the only family he had besides his uncle. He could do this.

He *had* to do this.

Step one: Stop picturing her naked.

Step two: Don't take advantage of her.

Step three: Take multiple cold showers.

Nick would destroy anybody who harmed Alyssa. He couldn't risk losing his best friend.

Because on some level he knew if he took Alyssa up on her offer, he would never be able to let her go. Because two weeks would never be enough. Not with Alyssa.

CHAPTER 3

*B*randt sat in his silver Range Rover, admiring the enormous rectangular windows and clean lines of the golden-sand-colored building. Tearmann House, the home for abused women and children he'd created to help those who couldn't protect themselves against parents, partners––the whole screwed up system.

To save them from living a life on the streets. The way he had.

Even as pride filled him, a pit weighed in his gut. He'd been such an ass to Alyssa Saturday night. For the last decade, hell, up until last Christmas, he'd always treated her like a friend and little sister. Considered her one of the best people he knew. And he'd done everything in his power to avoid contemplating sex and Alyssa together.

But after her stunning suggestion? For the last thirty-six hours, the picture of her naked and willing haunted him. Could he bail? Create some excuse to avoid her? Maybe let Scott, his project manager, handle the initial meeting?

He blew out a disgusted breath. He'd never been a coward or a liar—he yanked the door open and exited the car. Over the years, he'd perfected his casual-guy persona through necessity, and damn if he couldn't keep his shit together when he saw her again. Maybe he just needed to get laid, but somehow the only person he could imagine rolling in the sheets with was Alyssa.

And it wasn't going to happen. Could never happen. Hell, Nick had asked him to babysit. It was like asking the Big Bad Wolf to protect Little Red Riding Hood.

Little Red Riding Hood pulled up in her shiny BMW coupe next to him, almost running over his toes. He stepped back and walked around to the driver's side of her car.

She extended one slender leg out of the car, and he swallowed. Hard. She slid out, and every muscle in his body leaped to attention. Like a horny teenager.

Her tall, slender body was encased in some type of dress that may have looked businesslike on the hanger, but on her, simply emphasized her curves.

He was screwed––the next two weeks threatened to be interminable. Hell, a long few months until the center was completed.

Game face, dude. Put on the game face.

"Morning," he said and strode toward the center's double-door entrance.

She muttered something under her breath. Yeah, he was acting like a dick. Again.

He paused and waited for her to catch up. "Did Nick and Sophie get to the airport okay?" There. He sounded perfectly professional, friendly even.

"Yes, I dropped them off yesterday." Her mirrored aviator sunglasses hid her slate-blue eyes and her expression appeared neutral. Maybe she didn't hate his guts.

They approached the door and reached for the brass handle at the same time. When their fingers brushed, she stiffened and snatched her hand back.

"Let me." He could at least be polite, right?

Her soft pink lips flattened but she allowed him to open the heavy entrance door.

Unable to resist, he leaned down and inhaled the lemony fragrance of her long tawny hair. Why the hell did she have to smell so mouthwatering?

He was losing his fricking mind.

They entered what would become the lobby with its soaring twelve-foot ceilings and a sweeping staircase leading up to the second-floor residential rooms.

She stopped short. "Wow, it's enormous."

Because he was following her closely, he bumped into her. Tried to ignore the blast of heat through his system from her proximity.

"Must you stand so close to me?" She hissed.

"Sorry." He ground his molars together and struggled for self-control.

"Whatever." She stalked farther into the building on a pair of spiked heels that showcased her incredible legs. Sweat prickled along the back of his neck. Hell, he would never survive working with her.

His project manager appeared around the corner. "Hey, guys. Perfect timing. You must be Alyssa. I'm Scott, great to meet you." He extended his hand toward her.

"Oh, thanks so much. Nice to meet you, Scott. I'm looking forward to this project with you." She flashed her devastating smile.

Scott's face lit up like a child's on Christmas morning. Why the hell was he still holding her hand? Brandt ground his molars to dust.

Did women find the guy attractive? Sure, he was big and buff. He had to be a little too Venice Beach muscleman for Alyssa, didn't he?

"Do you want to take the tour first and see what's what or

go ahead and sit down with the plans?" Scott beamed at her like an idiot.

"Oh, I'd love to get a visual first so I can get a feel for it." Without a glance at him, she strolled down the corridor with Scott.

He trailed behind them like a third wheel. Or the invisible man. What the hell? Stop watching the sway of her hips and the way the dress shows off her perfect ass. Saturday night he'd had his hands on her sexy curves, and as if by rote memory, he was hard again.

Damn her for changing the playing field. Now she'd propositioned him, his usual self-control vanished. He started reciting calculus formulas in his head. Not that they'd bother to look at him, much less see the obvious bulge in his jeans.

"I love all the huge windows. It's so light and airy." She continued to speak only to Scott as if *he* owned the place or something.

Brandt forced one foot in front of the other and moved on to listing scientific formulas. Thank god they'd almost reached the conference room.

FROM THE MOMENT Alyssa had smacked the snooze button on the alarm clock trilling next to her head, she'd dreaded seeing Brandt today. After the most humiliating rejection of her life, she'd avoided him for the remainder of the reception, which fortunately hadn't featured a formal bridal party seating arrangement. Cocktails flowed and most guests-- not Brandt thank god--had spent the rest of the party on the dance floor.

And if she'd spent an hour in her walk-in closet last night and had laid out three potential outfits, shoes and all, it was only because she wanted to look cool, calm, and collected. Totally in control. She chose outfit number two: the blue wrap dress which happened to also make her look hot as hell. If she did say so herself.

Alyssa struggled to focus on Scott's commentary. Damn Brandt. His eyes bored holes into her back. What was his deal this morning? She'd give him the cold shoulder if it killed her.

And it just might.

If he were so attracted to her, he would've agreed to her offer, right? Since he'd shot her down in flames, he could at least have the decency to ignore her today. So why was he opening doors, hovering, and acting like a pest? Practically breathing down her neck. She could swear he'd sniffed her. *Sniffed her.*

Rude, infuriating man. Inhaling a steadying breath, she forced herself to concentrate on her brother's amazing design.

Sunlight streamed through the abundance of windows and imparted a feeling of freedom and space, perfect for the planned occupants. The building's high-ceilinged interior remained a shell because the team was waiting for her input on the specific room layout. Fresh ideas flooded her brain and anticipation filled her. Confidence in her artistic abilities wasn't the issue facing her on this project. She'd ensure Tearmann House's beauty and serenity.

Serenity. What a concept. *Ha.*

If only Brandt's presence didn't distract her so much. Ignoring him and listening to Scott took a herculean effort. Because his chilly rebuff haunted her. His detached words on eternal replay like a terrible broken record. Or nightmare.

"Let's head into the office," Brandt said from behind them.

If she wasn't mistaken, he sounded annoyed. Petty satisfaction filled her––served him right.

Without bothering to acknowledge him, she allowed Scott to escort her into the large conference room. A massive mahogany table and a few chairs dominated the room. Although the floors were unfinished and the walls were bare drywall, the open space held excellent potential.

"Can I get you a drink, Alyssa?" Scott headed to a small refrigerator against the far wall. "Water? Soda?"

Brandt smacked his computer and notebook onto the table, without a word. The tic in his jaw and his tense shoulders screamed his irritation.

She sat across from Brandt and bit her lip to stifle a giggle. "Water would be great. Thanks." Maybe working with Brandt would be fun, as long as Scott was around.

"I'll have water too. Thanks for asking." Sarcasm tinged Brandt's reply.

With a sheepish smile, Scott pulled three bottles of water out of the refrigerator and joined them at the table. "Sorry boss."

Without a word, Brandt powered on his laptop, looking too handsome with his carved-from-marble features and his chiseled lips pressed together. He glanced up and pinned her with his inscrutable gaze.

How could simply looking at him make every nerve-ending tingle? It was ridiculous and unfair.

Time to pull herself together. She straightened in her chair, smoothed her hair back, and opened her binder. "Give me a second to get organized."

"Sure, take your time." Scott's agreeable voice soothed her.

Not a peep from Brandt. Damn him.

She thumbed through her color-coded folder tabs, willing herself to shove Brandt into the back vault of her brain. She needed to get him out of her system and her two-week plan seemed perfectly reasonable to her. His reputation didn't concern her because her brother had been the same way-- on the surface neither man appeared to want to settle down. Why would you when you're gorgeous, rich, and successful?

But if Nick could fall madly in love and get married, couldn't she have the fairy tale too? Although, marriage and family with Brandt were about as likely as his sliding Cinderella's glass slipper onto her foot. But him not wanting a committed relationship didn't explain why he refused to sleep with her.

"Alyssa?" Scott's voice filtered in from a million miles away.

Color flamed up her cheeks. "Sorry, gentlemen. Let's get started."

CHAPTER 4

"So that's an overview of my concept. Can you tell me more about your vision to make sure I can create exactly what you want?" Alyssa gazed at him, sincerity gleaming in her gray-blue eyes.

Damn if her creativity and precision didn't make her even more attractive. He'd always admired her intelligence and knew she had graduated top of her class from Savannah College of Art and Design––but seeing her in a work setting was enlightening.

He paused and rubbed his jaw. "My number one priority is for it to feel welcoming and safe. Open, inviting, and not remotely institutional."

"Okay, got it. Open and airy, yet with a cozy feel. Warm colors, comfortable furniture…" This is good. Keep going." Alyssa typed notes.

"Think the women and children who can't or won't go to a shelter, who need a few days to regroup and make a plan. Many of these people are in transition—they've got nowhere else to go." His mind flashed back to his mother. What if she'd had a chance? Could it have changed her?

Unable to sit any longer, he surged to his feet and paced around the room. "Safe temporary housing for emergencies or short-term visitors. A room with computers where staff assist with finding jobs and access to job training. An old friend is working on getting business-clothes donations and volunteers to provide makeup and hairstyling to help give the women more confidence to start fresh."

Alyssa pressed one hand to her chest. "Brandt, this is incredible."

"Security will be airtight. They'll feel completely secure, without fear of whomever or whatever they were running from," Scott piped in.

Alyssa nodded and her fingers raced over her keyboard. She lifted a slender hand, gesturing for him to continue.

How much detail should he divulge? Especially with Scott sitting in on the meeting. He fiercely guarded his past. "Okay, I'm hiring a nurse practitioner for basic health needs and emergencies."

"Oh, I hadn't thought of that. Definitely a separate space. Still not facility-like, though. Keep going." She smiled, and his mind blanked. Damn, she was beautiful.

"Brandt?" A crease formed between her brows.

Shit. What was he talking about again? He paused behind his chair willing his brain to function. To focus on the kids.

"Sorry. The kids are my first priority. I want to provide a space where they feel wanted. Where they might be able to trust the idea the world isn't a transient place where adults let you down or, worse, harm you physically or emotionally. A world where they aren't their parents."

She frowned. "This sounds amazing and so necessary for these poor kids. Okay, so a playroom and maybe a library?"

"Exactly. A place where they can relax enough to feel like children." His hands curled around the back edge of his chair, and he struggled to lower his voice.

"I love seeing your passion for the center. I didn't realize you knew so much about the foster care system." She stopped typing and leaned forward; her gaze inquisitive.

He resumed his pacing. Very few people knew about his troubled childhood. He preferred it that way. Nobody would get the chance to judge or pity him.

Especially Alyssa.

"A lot of kids get lost in the system. So many foster homes are terrible, and kids feel like a burden even being there. Or sometimes the foster home is like jumping from the frying pan into the fire."

"Brandt, how awful. Aren't there good people working in the system?"

"Sure. And great foster parents." He shrugged, pausing to lean a hip against the table. "But there are cracks. Hell, huge craters, actually. Tearmann House is meant to bridge those gaps. Be the sanctuary, the safe haven to provide some hope."

"A sanctuary. We'll create it together here. Well, I've got the emotional aspect now, and that's huge." Her full pink lips curved into another warm smile. "Anything else? I'd like to head back to my office and integrate what we've discussed into my plans before tomorrow."

"I don't." He turned toward his manager. "Scott, you have anything?"

"Nope. I'm honored to be a part of this project. I've gotta run to a meeting. Again, great to meet you, Alyssa." Scott's moronic grin reappeared, and he backed out of the room with a wave.

Once they were alone, the air thickened. Damn it, one look at her and his mind snapped from let's save the children to peel-Alyssa's-dress-off mode. Time to downshift gears or run. Instead, he sat down.

"So…" She moistened her top lip with her tongue.

He stifled a groan. "So?"

"Well, now Scott's gone, can I ask a few more questions? I'd love to hear a little more about Tearmann House, like why that name?"

"Tearmann means safe haven in Gaelic, and I've got some Irish ancestors, so I figured I'd go with it." He shrugged.

"I know. I looked it up." She laughed when he quirked a brow. "I'm a total dork, okay? Can you tell me more about your connection to it?"

"Nick didn't share anything?" He hesitated, unsure of how much to reveal.

Once he'd hit it big in the tech world, he'd made damn sure nobody could dig up a speck of dirt about his past. As far as the world was concerned, he'd burst out of nowhere in his late teens. Only Nick and another friend, Christian, knew some of it. But he trusted Alyssa, and if she understood the more personal aspect of his motivation, she could incorporate the knowledge into her designs.

When she shook her head, he plunged in. "I lost my parents when I was nine and ended up in the system. Let's just say it was a rough ride."

"I'm so sorry. I had no idea. I hate thinking of you as a little boy alone in the world." She clasped her hands together.

He stiffened. "I'm fine. It was a long time ago." No way in hell would he stand for her picturing him as a lost little boy.

"You are, but I can still be sad for the child who lost his parents. I understand. I was fourteen when my parents were killed. We're kind of alike, then. Right? I was lonely. It's why I want lots of kids, and I hope Nick and Sophie do too." Her high cheekbones pinkened.

"Not really alike, babe. Your parents loved you. Mine, not so much." He kept his tone level even while bitter memories bubbled inside him.

One more reason he could never allow himself to get involved with her. He would never have kids. *Ever*. No way would he pass along the violent, defective genes his parents had passed along to him. Blood didn't lie. The Dempsey line stopped with him.

"So you had it rough before foster care too?" She searched his face, her eyes wide.

"Let's just say my parents weren't role models." Anger flared and he tamped it down. "Look, I swore one day I'd make a lot of money and give back and help other kids and women tossed around the system who end up on the street. So here we are."

Before she could read anything on his face, he pushed away from the table. Slipped on his poker face, the one he'd perfected before he'd reached his teens. He'd already divulged more than he'd planned. Something about Alyssa made him feel like he could be open––dangerous.

When he turned back toward her, she'd dug her white teeth into her plump lower lip again. He drew in a ragged breath.

She peeked up at him through her thick fringe of lashes. "I had no idea. I'm sorry. This center must mean so much to you."

"Are we done?" He bit out the words. Between wanting to kiss her and wanting her to stop looking at him with sympathy, he was about to lose it. Couldn't she see that?

"I'm sorry," she repeated and dropped her gaze. "I'll head out." She stood and stuffed her belongings back into her briefcase.

"Stop apologizing, damn it. It's over, and I turned out fine." The anger was winning. Nobody felt sorry for him. Period.

"Obviously, you're sensitive about this. I think what you're doing is amazing, and I'll do everything I can to help. No need for you to be so defensive." Her tone chilled, her posture rigid as she stalked away from the table.

"I'm not defensive." Right. He sounded like a petulant three-year-old boy who'd lost his favorite toy soldier.

"Fine. Whatever. You're not defensive. I've got to go." She brushed past him on the way to the door.

He caught her arm, unable to help himself. "Alyssa."

She attempted to shake off his hand, but he held on. "Don't touch me."

"You wanted me to touch you the other night." Every muscle in his body stiffened at the memory.

She dropped her briefcase and shoved him hard enough to send him stumbling back a few steps. "How dare you! After the way you rejected me? You made it clear you don't want me, so back off." A rosy blush stained her cheeks, and her hands curled into fists.

Something inside him snapped, and he grabbed her shoulders and yanked her against him. Her soft breasts smashed against his chest, her tart scent enveloped him, and once again, his mind emptied.

Screw it. He threaded his fingers through her hair and held her head in place, then slanted his mouth against hers.

After a split second, she wrapped her arms around his neck and her lips parted with a sigh. The sweet, honeyed taste of her tossed a match onto the fire raging inside him. He deepened the kiss. He could devour her right here on the spot.

HER HEART SLAMMED against her ribs and heat bloomed low in her belly as she surrendered to his punishing kiss. All she could do was hold on for the ride. One strong hand stroked down her jaw and throat, then palmed her breast. Her nipples pebbled immediately. His other hand cupped her bottom and pressed her hips into his arousal. From a distance, a moan pierced the quiet. Was that her?

With a growl, he backed them up until she was up against the conference table. Somehow the hand on her breast was inside her dress, and he pinched her aching nipple. Her hips jerked and slammed against his.

"Brandt, you taste so good," she murmured against his lips. He tasted like mint and something uniquely him. She couldn't catch her breath. What had she unleashed?

Lifting his head, he looked down at her, his pupils flared, his breath unsteady. He ripped off the belt holding her wrap dress together, and her top fell open, revealing her lacy push-up bra.

"So perfect..." He parted the fabric, tugging the lingerie down, freeing her breasts. His molten blue eyes never left hers as he brushed his thumbs back and forth.

Her heart hammered against her ribcage, and she couldn't tear her gaze away from his hands worshiping her curves. He lowered his head and closed his mouth over her breast. Flames shot straight down to her core. She gripped his firm biceps, reveling in his strength. Flying, she was flying.

He tugged on her nipple with his teeth, and rational thoughts scattered. The table digging into her back vaguely registered. He dragged her legs up and she wrapped them around his waist. They both moaned when his rock-hard erection connected with her burning center.

He lifted his head and kissed her again. His hands were everywhere, spanning her waist and then rolling her nipples between his fingers. Could she really be close to coming apart, just from his incredible hands and mouth? Usually, she had to concentrate—hard—to get where she needed to go.

He reached one hand down between them and cupped her, exerting a subtle pressure that only drove her closer to the edge.

"Baby, you're ready for me, aren't you?" He rasped and raked his teeth against her sensitive neck.

"Mmm…" Why was he talking?

"Tell me." He nibbled along her collarbone, his hand still. Teasing her.

"Yes…please." She rocked into his hand.

He added one finger, then a second. Lightning jolted to her core. He pressed his palm against her center again and propelled her over the edge. Tumbling into one of the most intense orgasms she'd ever experienced. Waves of ecstasy washed through her while he murmured her name against her lips, then grazed his nose along her jaw and kissed down to the hollow between her collarbones.

"God, you're so beautiful." He skimmed her hair back from her face.

She opened her eyes and met his heavy-lidded gaze. Overwhelmed by the passion simmering between them, her eyes fluttered shut. Was she really half-naked, on the conference table in Tearmann House with Brandt? Why did it feel so natural and right?

Nobody bossed her around. She'd cultivated her self-sufficient persona over the years since high school. But Brandt's domineering side excited her beyond belief. Her lips curved up as she basked in the afterglow.

The ringing of a phone on the table doused her fantasy like an icy bucket of water. Brandt froze.

"I think it's yours. Are you going to answer it?" Reality began to settle in.

"A minute ago you wouldn't have allowed any interruptions." His voice was husky, teasing. Despite his words, he eased back, drawing her dress together before he shifted to check his phone.

"Shit." He rubbed his hand across his jaw, grabbed the phone, and pivoted away from her.

"What? Who is it?" She stood and adjusted her dress. Lord knows what she must look like.

He flicked his gaze back to her. No longer blue fire, his eyes had chilled to chips of cerulean ice. "It's Nick."

Oh no. Thank god her brother hadn't used video calling. Damn her overprotective brother's radar. Make that icy bucket of water a torrential sleet storm. What now? She tuned in to Brandt's side of the conversation, but monosyllables weren't exactly enlightening.

He turned and looked back at her. His jaw was carved from granite. *Great. The Nick effect.*

"Yeah, she's still here. Here you go." He thrust the phone into her hand before she could protest.

"Hi, Nick. Is the honeymoon over already? I can't believe you're calling your first day?" Offense was the best defense with her big brother.

Nick laughed. "Honeymoon's great. I just wanted to make sure Brandt was keeping an eye on you like I asked."

Annoyance flared. "Seriously? Are you kidding me? You asked him to babysit me?" When would her Nick let go of the past and treat her like an adult?

"Can you blame me? After everything you went through?" Concern flowed through the connection.

"Nick, it has been years." Her fingers gripped the phone. "*Years.*"

"Sorry, sorry. I'll butt out." He managed to sound contrite.

"I love you, Nick, but I'm twenty-nine. Please don't worry. Give my best to Sophie. Buh-bye." She powered off the phone and turned toward her nanny, or was he a manny?

Brandt's posture was rigid as he packed up his things. His jerky movements didn't bode well. Uh- oh.

When she gave him the phone, she brushed her hand along his shoulder. He jumped as if he'd been shot. When he turned toward her, he remained just out of reach.

Her heart plummeted at his wooden expression. "Brandt? Are we going to talk about what happened?"

"I'm sorry. Nothing to discuss. It will never happen again." Without a backward glance, he raced out of the room.

She bent over the table, struggling to catch her breath. It was only Monday. They had spent mere hours together, with Scott in attendance no less, and already everything was imploding. Now what?

CHAPTER 5

$\mathcal{B}$randt did his best not to sprint out of Tearmann House, although at the pace he was moving, nobody could accuse him of dawdling. What the hell had just happened?

Besides the obvious––he'd lost his damn mind. Despite his best intentions, he'd manhandled Alyssa, and holy shit, what now?

Space. Miles of space.

He vaulted into his car and reversed out of the parking lot. He flew south on Coast Highway, desperate to reach his house. He'd just let Bailey out for a quick bathroom break and then hit the surf.

Clear his head.

Figure out his next move.

He turned up the meandering hill leading to his house. As the emerald-green trees grew denser and the town faded in the rearview mirror, the pit in his belly softened. For some reason, Alyssa's proposition had penetrated—oh, who the hell was he kidding, obliterated—his guard and he was a mess.

When he reached the tall wrought-iron gates, he pulled into his long curved driveway and flipped off the engine. His tense shoulders melted back into the leather seat, and he paused to admire his home. The first and only true home he'd ever had.

Over a decade ago, he'd stumbled upon this gem of a property. An old eccentric Hollywood actor had allowed the estate to deteriorate, just as he'd decayed through age and too much whiskey. Suffocating with weeds and peeling paint, the prior house also boasted a swimming pool the Loch Ness Monster probably used as a summer vacation spot.

Something about the property tugged at him, and he'd plunked down the cash. A new multimillionaire at the tender age of twenty-two, he'd figured why the hell not. The ruin was his second major purchase after the 1966 Corvette Stingray he'd lovingly restored to her former glory.

Around the same time, he'd met Nick in the surf lineup. An eager new architect, Nick had jumped at the chance to help him restore the old relic.

Despite the crumbling exterior, it was a noble structure and deserved another chance. They'd ripped the house down to the studs. Nick's brilliant design combined with Brandt's vision coalesced to create his own personal nirvana.

The house was the perfect marriage of wood and glass. Enormous front windows showcased breathtaking views of his beloved Pacific Ocean and the quaint seaside town he called home. He'd tried living in L.A., but the congested streets and concrete jungle choked him, reminding him of those early years in the rundown trailer park.

No—Laguna Beach was home.

Bounding up the stairs, he reached the front door and shoved it open. Bailey leaped upon him, slathering him with kisses. He buried his face in her soft coat. He'd considered adopting his own furry companion over the years. Too much responsibility. Borrowing his friend's dog was enough "parenting" for him.

Bailey trotted to the French doors on the opposite side of the great room and waited expectantly. Once he'd set her free, she did her business on the far side of the yard. By Southern California standards, the acre lot was enormous. The eclectic mix of majestic palm trees, sycamores, and even an ancient eucalyptus tree formed a soothing sense of seclusion.

He contemplated the restored swimming pool, which echoed the original Spanish style, with ornate tiles and an enormous curved shape. The sparkling water beckoned, but he craved the power of Mother Ocean, not the boundaries of enclosed walls.

After several rounds throwing a slobbery tennis ball for Bailey, Brandt escorted her back into the house for nap number five of her busy dog day.

He threw on a pair of board shorts and grabbed his rash guard. Time for the sun on his face, the waves beneath him, and the feeling of peace that permeated when he was in the water. Nothing else compared.

His Corvette looked inviting, so he tossed his short six-one board into it and cruised down to one of his favorite surf breaks off Thalia Street. Parking was easy for once, and he hit the surf.

An hour or so later, he climbed the steps to his car. He'd burned off a lot of energy in the pumping waves, which allowed a sliver of sanity to reenter his muddled brain.

On wave number seven of his session, he'd hatched a logical, foolproof plan. Go talk to Alyssa today. Communicate the ground rules for working together. No more touching, for one.

He'd be clear, calm, and reasonable.

A flash of movement caught his eye. Someone was sitting behind the wheel of his car.

He sprinted across the street toward his prized baby. "Hey! What the hell are you doing?"

The perpetrator leaped out of the Corvette and bolted down the street. *Shit.* He tossed his surfboard into the backseat, praying nobody would try to steal it too. But no way in hell was anyone getting away with messing with his 'Vette.

He chased the thwarted thief. He was small. Like-a-child small. Shit, the kid probably wasn't old enough to drive a car, much less try to steal one. The boy zigzagged down the street, but Brandt's anger fueled him to catch up. He snagged him by the back of his ratty green T-shirt.

The boy slithered out of the shirt and kept sprinting.

Little shit.

Brandt accelerated and caught the kid around his waist and hauled him back. Gangly arms flailed and landed a punch on his shoulder before Brandt grabbed his wrist and snaked his other arm too.

"Stop struggling. Stop. I've got you." The kid continued to squirm, but Brandt held tight. "Look, stop now, or I'm hauling you right down to the police station and they'll toss your delinquent ass into juvie."

The boy froze and looked up at him with a pinched face dominated by enormous root-beer brown eyes. Brandt's breathing slowed enough to take in the kid's whole demeanor. Skinny as a rail. Ragged jean shorts. No shoes. Damn it. He'd been racing down the sidewalk like a greyhound, barefoot.

The boy remained silent, shaking like a leaf now. Bruises were peppered all down the boy's arms. He recognized the signs. His heart sank. Damn it.

He'd been beaten.

"I'm not going to hurt you. I'm not going to take you to

the police. But what the hell were you doing?" He softened his tone and loosened his grip.

The kid shrugged a bony shoulder and stared at the sidewalk. "I wasn't doing nothing. Just checking out the sweet car. I was only looking."

"Yeah, sure you were. What's your name?" When the boy stayed silent, Brandt repeated his question.

"Kevin." The boy's eyes remained downcast.

"Look at me, Kevin."

No reaction.

"Let's go check out the car. I need to make sure nothing is out of place, and then you can go." Although if Kevin had ripped open his steering column...Brandt sighed.

Kevin marched beside him to the car. Brandt didn't see any obvious damage. Maybe the kid wasn't a grand-theft-auto felon in training, after all.

"Okay, everything looks okay." Brandt crouched down so they were eye to eye. "Look, you need to never do this again. You could be in custody right now or worse. Do you understand?"

The boy nodded.

"Let me give you a ride home. Where do you live?" Maybe he could see if his situation was safe.

Kevin stiffened, and his eyes widened. "No, no, mister. You don't need to give me a ride." He backed away.

Shit.

"Hold on." Brandt held up one hand, reached into the glove compartment, and grabbed a rumpled business card. He shoved it into the boy's hands and backed up a step. "Look, if you're in trouble, you can call me, okay? Or if you want to go for a spin in the Corvette, I'll give you one."

Kevin looked down at the card and raised his dark eyes. He turned and hightailed it down the street. Brandt sighed again as he watched him go, long-forgotten feelings twisting in his belly. He recognized the boy and his situation.

It was like looking at a mirror from the past.

AFTER MEETING KEVIN, Brandt's commitment to Tearmann House intensified, if that were possible. He wanted kids like him to have a place to go. Although the boy hadn't said much, Brandt could read between the lines.

Energized, he hurried home, showered, threw on some jeans and a T-shirt, and grabbed Bailey. She'd be a great buffer when he went to talk to Alyssa. God knew he needed one.

Much as he dreaded having the conversation, they needed to clear the air and return to solid footing. Chemistry be damned. No more pouncing on her. Although, her passionate response already haunted him.

He parked outside her condo––should he have called first? No, he needed to do this now.

He hadn't been to her new place and didn't know what to expect. He and Bailey walked up the exterior stairs of the buff-colored Spanish-style building that housed four units. When he reached her front door, he frowned. No security at all—anybody could walk up. Not safe.

Palms suddenly sweaty, he knocked on the door, secretly hoping she wouldn't be home because now that he was on her doorstep, his idea didn't seem so brilliant, after all.

The door cracked open, and Alyssa peeked out. The sight of her punched him in the gut. She was so damn beautiful, more beautiful than anyone had a right to be. Her sun-streaked blonde hair was scooped back into a high ponytail, and she was barely covered by some skimpy yoga-type clothing.

He swallowed--his throat dried out like the Mojave Desert. Yeah, definitely a terrible idea. What the hell had he been thinking?

She leaned against the doorjamb; arms crossed across her chest. She arched her eyebrows but didn't say a word.

"Can I come in? We need to talk." Had his voice just cracked like a teenager's?

"Talk?" She wrinkled her small nose. "Seriously?"

"Look, Alyssa, can I come in? I have some things to say to you." For Nick. For himself.

"Fine, come in." She spun away and ambled back into her apartment, leaving him to follow and shut the door.

He attempted not to stare at her tight little butt framed flawlessly in her snug white leggings. With effort, he lifted his gaze and checked out her place. No surprise—it felt homey and open. Warm caramel colors, whites, and accents of turquoise blue created a perfect backdrop for her tawny blonde beauty.

Damn it. It also smelled like her. Hints of grapefruit and citrus. Mouthwatering.

He was in big trouble.

hy was he here? After the way he'd bolted out of the building, she assumed he'd avoid her forever, or at least until Nick was back in town. Alyssa practiced her yoga breathing on the short stroll to her living room, trying to soothe her nervous system. Inhale for four, hold for four, exhale for four.

Her pulse hammered in her throat––she hadn't yet fortified her defenses after the passionate scene earlier. Certainly not up for a mature conversation. She sank into the cushions of her L-shaped cocoa-brown sofa, tucked her legs underneath her, and forced herself to breathe slow and steady.

Brandt sat opposite her in the matching oversized chair. "We need to set some ground rules for working on this project." His hands gripped his knees. Although his expression was composed, his knuckles were white.

"Rules?"

He nodded. "Rules. We need to be professional. Shit, your brother asked me to watch over you while he was gone, and then this happens."

The more he squirmed, the easier her breath flowed. *"This?"*

His fingers gripped his legs tighter, and his face paled under his bronzed skin. Fascinating.

He shot out of the chair and stalked around the room like a restless caged lion. Pacing was obviously one of his tells. And, god, he was so hot, especially now his usual surfer-guy cool was nowhere in sight.

Damn it. She'd remind him she wasn't his baby sister. Their chemistry was explosive. Over the top. But she wanted a chance with him and not just for his sculpted six-pack abs. She wanted Brandt for what lay beneath the surface. The real man behind the mask.

Because the real reason she'd fallen for him all those years ago? Not just because he was the most beautiful man she'd ever seen, and he was nice to her.

But because one afternoon when she was seventeen, he'd saved her from a group of bullies at the beach. She'd been hanging out reading a book, minding her own business, when a pack of the local surf punks started making fun of her. Calling her names. Taunting her. Telling her that ugly girls like her shouldn't hang out on their turf but should go to the pound with the other dogs.

When they wouldn't stop, she'd run on trembling legs to the steep cliff stairs and tripped. Suddenly, Brandt had appeared out of nowhere, still in his wetsuit, his face ablaze with fury. He'd dealt with the kids, who scurried off like little rats. And he'd sat with her until he was convinced she was fine. His protectiveness and sweetness had ignited love in her lonely young heart. Nobody besides her brother had ever stood up for her before.

Sure, the bullies had been awful, but she'd been accustomed to the mean girls in boarding school. What Brandt hadn't known was she'd been struggling with her inner demons. He'd thought the shivers racking her body were from being upset, not from another self-imposed hunger strike. Nobody knew about her darkest secret, and they never would. Through therapy, she'd been healthy for years now.

The mass of knots in her belly unfurled. "Okay, are you referring to tearing my dress off in the conference room and bending me over the table? Or the fact that if the phone hadn't rung, I wouldn't have been the only one feeling relaxed right now?"

"This isn't how I expected you to act." Brandt's mouth dropped open.

Was he shocked and maybe even a little embarrassed? She bit her lip to hide her smile. "We're even then because after you turned me down the other night, I didn't expect you to rip my dress off today."

He opened and closed his mouth a few times, appearing at a loss for words. Mr. Brandt Dempsey wasn't immune to her. Not at all. His walls were high, but they weren't impenetrable. The more time she spent with him, the more convinced she was that the only solution to their dilemma was to hook up. See where this explosive chemistry could lead. It just had to seem like his idea.

She shrugged a shoulder. "Okay, truce. I was just starting to make dinner. Why don't you stay, and we'll discuss whatever you want like civilized adults over a meal."

She stood and reached for his hand, unable to prevent a smile.

He glanced down at their intertwined fingers but didn't withdraw. "I don't know if that's a good idea..."

"Seriously? Are you scared you can't control yourself over dinner? We've been friends for years, right?" She laughed and released him.

Without waiting for a reply, she turned and strolled into

the kitchen. Her prized Le Creuset skillet sat ready for action, along with an Alaskan king salmon steak she'd planned to sauté with some steamed zucchini and red peppers. The fish portion was small, but she could toss in some quinoa and stretch it into a meal for two.

"Wow, this is a true chef's kitchen. So you love to cook, then?" He stood in the doorway, looking around the kitchen.

Alyssa studied her favorite room. It was large, with gray-and-white-marbled granite countertops, stainless steel appliances, white cabinets, and a gorgeous backsplash of varying shades of brilliant blue. An island framed with tall barstools dominated the center of the room, making it a perfect place to hang out.

"I do. I prefer baking actually, but I try to control myself. I don't need to eat batches of cookies and cupcakes on a regular basis. Do you want a glass of wine? I've got a great Sonoma chardonnay." She pulled a bottle out of the huge refrigerator.

He shrugged and leaned against the center island. "I guess. And I could eat."

When she gave him the bottle and corkscrew, she stroked her fingers down his muscular forearm. Brandt yanked his hand away as if he'd been burned.

No, not immune to her in the least.

He poured them two glasses and reached down to scratch Bailey's head. "What else can I do?"

"Bailey's water bowl is in the lower cabinet next to the sink. Can you fill it up and put it under the window please?"

He complied, then leaned against the counter and watched her add olive oil, garlic, and pepper to the salmon, and she started the water to steam the veggies. The sizzling aroma filled the air.

Her mind drifted off to a future where every night they could hang out and make dinner together. Have their own dog at their feet. A baby with Brandt's wavy, dark hair and big sapphire eyes.

Her hand jerked, and she brushed the side of the pan, scalding her fingers. She jumped back from the stove. "Ouch."

"Are you all right?" Brandt steered her to the sink, flipped on the cold water, and stuck her hand under it.

"Ouch, ouch, ouch. It stings." So much for her powers of seduction. "I'm such a klutz. Can you get me some ice and turn off the stove, so the fish doesn't burn?"

"Yeah, keep your hand under the water." He hurried around the kitchen, switching off the burners and throwing an ice pack together.

When he returned, he pressed the cold compress onto the scarlet welt emerging on her hand. The warmth of his breath and his clean beachy scent filled her nostrils. His proximity mesmerized her. The burn was forgotten as heat spread to different parts of her body.

"Is that okay?" He lifted his head and sucked in a breath. His pupils darkened; the irises narrowed to cerulean haloes.

Her breath lodged in her throat. Would he close the distance and kiss her?

He released her hand and retreated to the large window. Her breath whooshed out, and she gripped the ice pack to help her cool off.

In that split second of awareness, she'd been sure he'd kiss her. Baby steps. He wanted her. Time to play it cool and return to her initial plan of sharing a meal.

"I'm fine. Let me finish making dinner. Can you grab some plates and silverware and set them up on the island?" Alyssa injected lightness into her tone.

When he nodded and accommodated her requests, his poker face was back in place.

She plated the salmon and vegetables, quickly sliced up a

baguette she'd picked up the evening before and placed it in a dish between their settings.

"Let's eat."

"This looks incredible. Thanks." He smiled at her and sampled the fish.

They ate in companionable silence. Again, Alyssa marveled at how natural it felt to share a meal with him in her kitchen. If only he weren't so stubborn. At first she figured his reluctance to hook up with her was because of his friendship with Nick, but then he'd shared more about his personal motivation for Tearmann House. Maybe his rough childhood was another reason for his hesitancy.

Brandt never discussed his family or upbringing. In fact, now she considered it, she couldn't remember him talking about the past at all. Although he was famous in the tech world for his invention of Garda, his innovative cybersecurity firewall protection system, his life before his career remained shrouded in mystery. It was almost as if he'd been hatched in college, materializing out of thin air. Whatever his reluctance stemmed from, his rejection triggered her own memories of loss.

When their parents died, Nick was in college at Cornell in New York, and she'd been about to start high school in California. With no other relatives, Nick was appointed her guardian and she'd moved to New York, where she'd attended a private girls' boarding school. Or the seventh ring of hell.

They taunted her for being the outsider geeky brainiac. Many of the girls were obsessed with perfection. Perfect grades. Perfect hair. Perfect bodies. So during her freshman year of high school, she learned more by observing those girls as they put food on their plates and never touched it. Their self-control.

The pressure to fit in won out over her fragile self-esteem. She became obsessed with getting a handle on something in her life. She couldn't control how the other girls treated her. She couldn't bring her parents back, but she learned she could control what she put in her mouth.

Or at least she'd believed that would help her, once upon a time.

"Earth to Alyssa, where'd you go?" Brandt asked, jolting her back to the present.

"Sorry about that. Just a little tired, I guess." No need to rehash the horrible memories. She loved her life now--she'd built a great career and she loved Laguna Beach--and Brandt didn't need to hear more about her difficult years. He had his own demons.

Time to regroup and return her focus to what she wanted in the present moment. She picked up their plates and headed to the sink. He helped clear the rest of the dinner dishes. "Alyssa."

"Brandt?" She turned, offering him a hint of a smile.

A line etched between his brows. "I came over to talk to you about what happened today, so let's go sit down in the living room."

"I really don't think—" And they were back to his poker face. Somehow it didn't feel like he was about to seduce her.

"You wanted to talk earlier. So, please hear me out."

She shrugged and followed him to the living room. Like she had a choice without being even more awkward. Bailey lifted her head, cracking one eye open, probably checking for treats or a walk. When neither seemed imminent, she returned to her nap.

Alyssa sank onto the chair, and he sat on the far edge of the sofa. Way too far away. "Well?"

"Look, we just need to get through this project without a repeat of this afternoon." Scratching his jaw, he looked out the window before looking back at her.

No way was she making this easier for him. She gestured with her hand for him to continue.

"I know there's some chemistry between us..."

She rolled her eyes and grinned. "Some? Seriously? I mean, if we're having a talk, at least be accurate."

His nostrils flared and his hands were back to gripping his denim-clad thighs. "Fine, a lot. But that's not the point, okay?"

"So now you admit you are attracted to me. That was all b.s. Saturday night, wasn't it?" She smirked.

He huffed out a breath. "Let me finish. This is how it's going to be."

"We'll maintain our professional relationship. We'll act like normal around your brother. We'll pretend this never happened." He ticked off the points with his fingers. His long, talented fingers.

Could he be any cuter?

"Why? Why can't we be professional at work and get this out of our system at home? It's the perfect solution. I don't know why you're making something simple so difficult." Despite her confident words, a sliver of unease danced along her skin--she could handle it, right?

He scrubbed a hand across his face. "That's not the point..."

"Yes, it is. We're both adults, Nick is out of town for two weeks, and we're both attracted to each other. It seems simple to me." *Mostly.*

Sweat popped up on his forehead. "It is definitely not simple. Look, you aren't the kind of girl..."

"How do you know what kind of girl I am?" She leaned forward and her breasts strained against the fabric of her tissue-thin tank top.

His gaze was definitely over her left shoulder. Anywhere but at her face and body. "We have too much history, and I'm not willing to risk my relationship with Nick or Tearmann House to satisfy an itch."

Enough. "An itch? You act like I'm trying to steal your virtue or something." Alyssa approached and knelt in front of him. "Aren't you curious? Nobody will know—it'll be our secret. I know you have secrets. Can't you compartmentalize this one?"

Every muscle in Brandt's body sprang to attention. The visual of Alyssa on her knees in front of him? Like a modern-day Eve with the proverbial apple. Was she trying to kill him? But hell, he would die a happy man.

When he'd helped ice her burned hand, there'd been a moment when her proximity almost shattered his resolutions. Somehow over the course of the relaxed meal, his urgent need to institute rules with her had evaporated. But when she'd disappeared with a faraway look in her eyes, it snapped his brain back into place.

Alyssa Morgan wasn't a girl to have a fling with, she was the type you brought home to meet your parents. Well, other guys would do that--people with regular families. If they hooked up, it would be a relationship and that simply couldn't happen. He didn't do relationships.

Could he lock away an affair with her in the vault like she'd suggested? Hell, his entire life was based on a web of secrets, each buried deeper than the next. How tough could it be?

He spoke through gritted teeth, struggling to maintain a tenuous thread of control. "Alyssa, this is a really bad idea."

"I think it's a great idea." She shifted closer, slid one hand up his thigh, and pressed her breasts against him.

His self-control shattered. He shifted, grabbed her waist, and pulled her up to straddle his lap. Groaned at the feel of her hot center against his hard cock. He snaked one hand into her hair, held her head in place, and crushed his mouth to hers.

She purred her pleasure and returned his kiss as fiercely as he gave, teeth and tongues slamming into each other. She tugged his hair, sending sparks down his spine. Her long lean thighs gripped him tight, and the taste and feel of her jolted through him.

He freed Alyssa's fragrant hair from the ponytail, and it cascaded around them, creating a golden curtain as they devoured each other.

She dug her fingernails into his scalp, and the little frisson of pain drove him wild. Her little moans nearly sent him over the edge. He needed to see her, needed to touch her silky skin. He yanked her top up, whipped it over her head and across the room. He sucked in a breath at the vision of her creamy breasts, her perfect rosy nipples.

Her pupils dilated, and her blue eyes were almost black with desire. Her pink lips parted, and she panted in anticipation. He spanned her ribcage and pulled her closer. Flicked his tongue across a taut nipple. She jerked back with a moan, and he tightened his grip.

"You're not going anywhere now, beautiful." He took her in his mouth and fought the urge to swallow her whole. He'd never tasted anything so delicious.

"More." She demanded and arched her spine to give him fuller access.

No way in hell he could hold back now. Not with his

mouth on her. She rocked against him, creating intense friction, and damn if he didn't almost lose control. And when no more barriers existed between them?

And then Alyssa murmured against his lips. "Now, Brandt, now."

Hell yes, he wanted to be inside her right now. "So eager… Baby, you're driving me crazy."

He gripped her hips and flipped her, so she was on her back.

"Hold on and let me look at you." He groaned––with her hair wild and tangled around her face, her cheeks flushed, and her eyes heavy-lidded, she was a dream.

Something tugged in his chest. "You are the most beautiful woman I've ever seen."

"I want to see you." She grabbed his T-shirt and tugged. He reached back with one hand and tore it off.

Her breath caught and she trailed one hand down his pecs, to his abs, down to the bulge in his jeans. "Brandt. Please… I want you inside me so badly. Now." She curled her fingers around the top of his pants.

With a growl, he caught her hands and pressed them overhead. Leaned down and caught her mouth again, the feel of her like hot silk. She wrapped her legs around his back. Time to feel every single inch of her bare against him.

He released her hands, rolled to the side, and slid her yoga pants off. He kept his gaze locked with hers as he traced his fingers from her breast down to the edge of her panties. Little tremors ran over her soft skin. When he dragged her lacy thong down, she bucked into his hand.

"Brandt, please…" She stroked his arm, his shoulder, whatever she could reach. She wanted him now.

He nibbled down the velvety skin on the underside of her breast, trailed kisses along the curves and hollows of her body until he reached her sweet center. He blew lightly along the sensitive pink flesh.

"Is this what you want, beautiful?" He looked up at her from underneath his lashes.

"Damn it, yes!" Her hips rocked restlessly from side to side.

His lips curved up and he licked her in one long stroke. Fuck, she tasted like heaven. Within seconds they'd found a rhythm and she gripped his hair and rocked against his face. She came apart with a scream. He gripped her hips, holding her still until the waves rocking through her stilled and she went limp.

He needed to be inside her. *Now.*

With a growl, Brandt slid up her body, yanking his jeans down as he went, and pulled a condom out of his wallet. When she reached down and helped sheath him, he almost lost himself again. He caught the back of her legs and nudged them further apart.

He slid deep inside her wet heat until she'd taken every inch. He gripped one thigh and released the other. She wound her leg around his back and her back bowed up. "You feel so good. Ohmygod."

He took her in long powerful strokes, and she matched his pace as if this was the hundredth time they'd been together, not the first. Their skin grew slick and slippery and the sounds of their bodies slapping together filled the room.

He reached one hand between them and stroked her where they were joined. "Come for me now, baby."

"Now," he repeated, his words urgent against the side of her neck. He wasn't going to last much longer, his lower back beginning to tingle and burn.

She came apart with his name on her lips, and he flew over the edge with a roar. He dropped his head into the sweet hollow of her neck and collapsed.

He couldn't move.

He didn't want to move.

He'd somehow crossed the pearly gates into heaven.

Alyssa was heaven. She was more. More than he'd ever experienced. Incredibly responsive. Passionate. Sweet. Perfect. Like home. In fact, as she began to stroke his hair, he almost purred like a cat.

He jolted. Purr like a cat? What the hell? He started to shift away from her, but she tightened her grip and pressed her soft lips against his temple.

Relax, don't freak out. He could handle this. Of course, he could handle this. She was just another woman.

He turned his head and slanted his mouth across hers. He propped himself up on one forearm, so he didn't crush her. He rolled to the side and pulled her on top of him—because he wasn't ready to let her go.

And crashed them both onto the floor with a thump.

"Ouch." She scooted backward, tucking her long legs in front of her, and lifting an arm to cover herself.

"Alyssa, I'm so sorry. This was a…" Talk about jolting back to earth. No longer enveloped in their cozy afterglow, reality seeped in. What had he just done?

"Don't you dare apologize. This was incredible, and you know it. Don't ruin it." Her voice was soft, her eyes wide with a hint of vulnerability in their smoky depths.

She rose and reached out with one hand. "Let's go to my bedroom."

Despite her fear he'd freak out again, she continued to ask for what she wanted. She had to be the most courageous woman—hell, the most courageous person—he'd ever met.

If she could handle it, so could he.

And he was already on the direct trajectory to hell, so why fight it?

He threaded his fingers through hers and tugged her

down onto the lush carpet. She landed on top of him, and he pressed her soft, warm curves into him. Yeah, he was ready for her again. Already.

"Wow, so soon?" she smiled against his lips. "Who am I to say no?"

They were both eager. Hot. Passionate. Round two on the rug was just as incredible as round one. Maybe round three came with a bed.

BRANDT BLINKED the sleep from his eyes and brushed away the strands of wheat-blonde hair wrapped around him. What the hell? He closed his eyes and then popped one open. No, he wasn't dreaming. He'd spent the night with Alyssa.

She was draped around him, her head nestled into his chest, one slender arm thrown across his waist, and one leg flung across his. Pinning him down.

What had they done? His lips curved up of their own volition. What hadn't they done? He stiffened at the memory of the couch, the floor, and finally her bed. He couldn't deny it—last night had been the most amazing night of his life.

With his best friend's baby sister. Whom he was supposed to protect. Shit, shit, shit.

His heart slammed against his ribs. He needed to escape. Now. He eased Alyssa's arm off his chest, slowly sliding away from her inch by inch. So much for his brilliant idea of conveying the ground rules.

"Mmm…" she muttered as her leg tightened around his and she snuggled her face deeper against him.

He paused, holding his breath. Tried to control the shallow racing of his pulse. Once he'd ascertained she was still asleep, he continued his slither-and-stop routine until he'd untangled himself. With an adorable snort, she nestled into the pillow and continued to sleep.

Thank God.

Don't look at the expanse of silky golden skin.

Time to go.

Maybe this one night was enough to get the chemistry out of their system and move on as if nothing had happened. No way in hell could it happen again.

They had a few weeks until Nick returned, and by then, surely, all of this would be a distant memory. A hot memory, yes, but a memory.

Brandt tiptoed out of the bedroom, rubbing his jaw. Where were his clothes? When he reached the living room, he winced at the cyclone they'd left behind last night. Clothes, shoes, sofa pillows on the floor—chaos.

He snatched up his jeans and stuffed his legs in without bothering to find his boxers first. He needed to leave before she woke up. Regroup. Fortify his defenses.

Where the hell was his T-shirt?

Bailey jumped up and trotted over to him with her tail wagging, ready to go outside for her morning routine. Her tags jingled against her collar.

"Shhh, girl. Be quiet." He leaned down, held the metal tags still with one hand, and scratched her ears. Why couldn't all females be so simple?

"Brandt?" Alyssa's husky voice asked from behind him.

He turned toward her, his gut clenching at the puzzled look in her eyes. She'd wrapped the comforter around her like a toga, her tawny mane tangled around her incredible face.

"Oh, hey, um…I didn't want to wake you up. I've got some things to handle this morning." Sweat broke out on his brow. His bumbling sounded lame. He spotted his T-shirt underneath the armchair.

"Are you seriously sneaking out of here? After last night?" Her tone chilled.

"I'm not sneaking. I just…" Shit.

She yanked her makeshift toga tighter and hugged her arms around her waist. "Oh, give me a break. You're sneaking out like I'm some chick you met in a bar whose name you don't remember. I thought you were better than that."

"No, no, I just wanted to let you sleep, and I really do have someplace to be." His nose was growing.

"Get out." She bent down and picked up his boxers—how had they gotten all the way over there? —and hurled them at him. "Take these with you."

"Alyssa…" What could he say? He should just go.

It was better this way.

"Don't bother. I don't want to hear it." She pivoted on her heel and returned to her bedroom, slamming the door behind her.

Brandt snatched up his shorts, snaked the T-shirt, and grabbed Bailey's leash. He slunk out of the condo like the asshole he was.

CHAPTER 8

When the front door clicked shut, Alyssa slumped against the bedroom wall. Burying her face in her hands, she slid down the wall to the floor and smacked her head against her knees. Her stomach churned and she struggled to swallow the bile rising in her throat.

Last night's reality with Brandt had eclipsed her dreams. How could she have known how strong he'd feel? How perfectly they'd fit together? How deliciously clean and masculine he smelled up close and naked?

Damn it, last night hadn't been simple sexual chemistry. No, their connection went deeper. They had a foundation together. He'd been her knight in shining armor once when she'd been a fragile girl struggling with her emotional and physical health. Couldn't he be one again?

It wasn't like he could deny their chemistry now. And his eyes had held more--a hint of something deeper in the azure depths, vulnerability and affection. After last night, she'd assumed she'd have two weeks with Brandt to show him how they could build on their friendship and their chemistry. Show him how good they could be together.

And sure, it wasn't a secret he was afraid of intimacy—she'd never seen him with the same woman twice. But he cared about her, and up until the Mistletoe incident, he'd acted like it. Years of knowing each other, trusting each other, being family of a sort.

Okay, maybe she was stretching a teensy bit, but he and Nick were like brothers. She squeezed her eyes shut and dropped her head back against the wall when the image of her brother popped into her mind. Nick. The colossal thorn in her side.

Nick had also kept women at arm's length until he'd fallen head over heels. Sophie's love healed his heart from the abandonment issues stemming from losing their parents at such a young age. It hadn't been like her brother was incapable of love and commitment, he'd been scared. If he could overcome his fears, couldn't Brandt?

Not in one night, apparently. And if he'd already sprinted out the door, so much for two weeks to assure him they could sway her ridiculously overprotective brother's opinion. Two weeks to allow him time to fall in love with her. Fantasy officially shattered.

Anger poured through her—couldn't he have been mature enough to wake up together and have breakfast like a regular couple? What an ass—to not even wake her up and say goodbye after their mind-blowing night. Instead, he'd dashed out as if he couldn't wait to put miles between them.

So much for being different than all the other women he slept with. She rubbed the ache in her chest, fury battling with hurt. What now? A tear slid down her cheek, and she swiped it away. No, no, no. Anger was better than sadness and no way would she sit here and mope for him.

Maybe she could play hooky, as she had in grade school when she'd felt unprepared to face the day?

Fat chance.

Hadn't she been the one to suggest a purely physical affair? Time to practice what she'd preached. Or at least tuck away last night and shift her focus to Tearmann House.

Alyssa tap-danced through an ice-cold shower. Focused on the basics: soap, shampoo, and conditioner, then forced down a vat of coffee. She'd put on her game face, but breakfast was out of the question. Not a chance she could hold anything solid down. Pressing her hand against her jittery stomach, she moved through her morning routine.

Don't think. Just do.

She scraped her hair into a severe chignon, threw on a pair of navy narrow-leg trousers and a crisp white button-down shirt, and added her favorite scarlet stilettos for confidence. Nodding in approval at her reflection in the mirror, she attempted a smile. More like a grimace, but at least she looked businesslike and serious.

The opposite of how Brandt had seen her last.

Time to gather her strength and behave like a professional.

Despite the hollow ache in her belly.

WHEN SHE ARRIVED at Tearmann House, she exhaled a shaky breath––Brandt's car wasn't out front, thank god.

Okay, she could do this. She loved her career. She loved this project. Becoming a successful interior designer had fulfilled her for years. She could work despite feeling raw and ripped apart from Brandt's hasty departure this morning. *Jerk.*

After a few cleansing breaths, she headed inside.

Scott popped his head out of the conference room and grinned. "Hey, Alyssa, you're just the person I've been waiting for. Ready to review some timelines and set up a schedule?"

At least somebody was happy to see her this morning. Scott probably would have made her breakfast in bed and driven her to work. Too bad she wasn't attracted to him.

"Good morning. Sure, I'm ready. Let's do it." She injected enthusiasm into her voice.

Work was the answer. She could control where she directed her attention and she'd focus on her career, even if she could still feel the soreness between her thighs from last night.

She followed Scott into the conference room and unpacked her files and laptop onto the large table. Her throat tightened at a flash of Brandt bending her over said table. Annoyed with her one-track mind, she forced the memory aside.

No more obsessing over Mr. Brandt Dempsey.

His project manager chose the seat right next to her, instead of one of the other seven available chairs. Why was he invading her personal space? She resisted the urge to scoot away from him.

"Is anyone else joining us, or can we get started?" Brandt likely wasn't going to show. Not after this morning.

"Nope, just us. Brandt let me know he couldn't make it in —some meetings or something up in L.A. today." Scott shrugged.

She inclined her head. "Great. Let's put a rough timeline together and start planning out the teams who will come in and implement."

Hmm…did that mean Brandt hadn't been making excuses to get out the door this morning? Maybe he actually did have an important meeting. Or was he lying to Scott to make his story seem more authentic? She gave an internal eyeroll. So much for her unwavering focus on work.

"Let's do it." Scott nodded.

Methodically, they reviewed the sketches and plans and coordinated tentative deadlines onto a master calendar. Scott was bright and full of helpful suggestions and tweaks. Perhaps this job would be a smooth one, after all.

As long as Brandt didn't show up.

"Wow, it's late. Let's go grab some lunch." Scott closed his laptop.

"Oh no, I'm actually fine. I had a huge breakfast." She crossed her fingers under the table at the lie. "Why don't you go? I'll reorganize some of these details we've reviewed."

"We've been at it all morning. Can I at least bring you something back? You're already as skinny as a supermodel." His brows drew together.

Hackles rose up her spine. "Don't worry about what I'm eating—not really your business." She looked down at the files, dismissing him.

"Uh, just trying to be nice. If you change your mind, text me." He exited with a wave.

She dropped her head into her hands and closed her eyes. Why did people think they could make comments on when and what she ate? On how thin she was? Nobody would monitor her eating habits anymore, not like the program she'd gone through to get a handle on her former eating disorder where every bite was recorded and assessed.

At this point, she couldn't consume a morsel if she tried because she was devastated. Yes, simple garden-variety devastation. What else could it be when you caught the only man you'd ever loved sneaking out of your apartment after an incredible night together?

Nobody would be able to eat after the night she'd just had with Brandt and the way he'd ended it. It was natural to be upset. She swallowed the trickle of worry. Definitely not an eating disorder resurrecting its ugly head. Absolutely not.

Work now. Food later.

THIRTY HOURS, sixteen minutes, and possibly eleven seconds since Brandt flew out of her condo with the hounds of hell on his heels. Not that she was keeping count or anything.

Here she sat in the Tearmann House conference room—he'd managed to avoid her and Tearmann House—for thirty hours, seventeen minutes, and...*Damn it.*

She shook her head to stop her obsessing. He couldn't avoid her forever, could he? He wouldn't abandon his passion project simply to maintain distance between them. And, with Nick being his best friend, the chance of him avoiding her forever was slim to none.

She twisted a strand of hair around her finger, willing her nerves to settle. Her stomach rumbled, but she'd been unable to force herself to eat. Right now she was running on caffeine fumes. Her stomach growled again, jolting her back to awareness. Nausea or not, she needed to get a grip.

What was she doing? How had she allowed his behavior to relegate her to the psyche of a lonely sixteen-year-old girl with an eating disorder? No way would she relive her hellish high school years all over again.

Monitoring what she did or didn't put in her mouth used to give her some semblance of control over her life. Years of counseling taught her control was just an illusion. Consuming a plate of lasagna wasn't going to bring Brandt back. Abstaining from eating certainly wouldn't cause him to appear out of thin air either.

She tossed her pen down and rose from the conference table. Although she knew everything would taste like sawdust, she'd shovel lunch down her throat, even if it choked her.

Fresh air and food would exorcise him from her mind. For now. At some point, they'd have to act like adults and discuss what happened. Wouldn't they?

He couldn't just pretend things hadn't changed.

Could he?

CHAPTER 9

*H*iding out for a few days hadn't worked out too well for him. He'd avoided Tearmann House. Evaded Alyssa. When had he turned into such a damned coward?

The cool Pacific water usually soothed him, but today, not so much. Another towering wave approached, and he paddled to catch it and for a blissful few moments, rode into shore. The minute he hopped off his surfboard, his annoying brain began to whir again with the incessant Alyssa loop.

No amount of crisp salt air, warm sunshine, or punishment from Mother Ocean made a whit of difference. He trudged the last few feet through the whitewater, reached down to release his ankle leash, and tossed it around his surfboard.

"Hey, mister." Kevin's dark eyes looked ancient in his pinched young face.

Brandt shoved the hair out of his eyes and there was the boy who'd tried to hotwire his vintage Corvette, standing at the base of the stairs leading up to the street.

"Hey, Kevin, what's up?" He injected calm into his voice.

What was the kid doing at the beach alone——why wasn't he in school?

The boy shrugged. Barefoot, his clothes were rumpled and about a half size too small. At least, Brandt couldn't discern any obvious bruises or marks on him. A positive sign.

"I'm heading back to grab a burger. Wanna come?" He smiled gently at the boy.

Kevin shrugged again but fell into step beside him. They ascended the steep stairs together. When they reached the Corvette, Brandt popped the trunk and grabbed a beach towel, wrapped it around his waist, and pulled on a pair of board shorts.

After he'd changed, he gestured for the silent boy to hop in the front seat. "You okay with me giving you a ride? Ruby's Diner is a few miles down the road. But we can go some-where else and walk if you want." He didn't want to scare Kevin.

"Ride's cool." He clambered into the passenger seat and fastened the seat belt across his pint-sized lap.

Brandt eased the car onto the PCH and glanced over. The boy stared out the window, the warm breeze from the open convertible top ruffling his dark hair. He still hadn't really spoken, so Brandt would wait. Kevin had shown up for a reason, and he'd give him space to relax.

They cruised a few miles to South Laguna, and he turned into Ruby's Diner. The kid would like the old-fashioned atmosphere, and god knew he needed a giant burger and milkshake. He was borderline emaciated.

A bottle-blonde waitress sporting a skintight uniform led them to a shiny vinyl booth. She leaned down and handed them menus and fluttered her ridiculous false eyelashes at him.

"She wants to do it with you," Kevin said as the waitress sashayed to the next table.

"Naaah. She's just being friendly." He shook his head, although he had seen the obvious, emphasis on obvious, invitation on her face. *Crap.* Not what this boy needed to see.

"Right." Kevin smirked. "I bet you get tons of chicks with that car."

Brandt swallowed. Time to change the direction of this conversation. Pronto. "Anyway. So what's going on? Why aren't you at school?"

Kevin stared at his menu, suddenly laser-focused on the twenty hamburger choices. "I didn't have school today."

"Huh. Well, okay. But what you were doing at the beach?" Skipping school was a warning sign––he should know.

Kevin traced a thin finger along the edge of the laminated menu, revealing dirt crusted beneath the nail. "I saw your car. I figured I'd see if you were any good at surfing."

"I rip. What about you, grommet?" He'd seen tons of athletic kids out in the surf making the adults look like amateurs. It was an advantage to be small and wiry. Although he doubted Kevin had access to a surfboard. That is unless he stole one.

"Nah." Kevin didn't meet his eyes.

The waitress returned, and they both ordered double cheeseburgers, fries, and chocolate milkshakes. Lunch of champions.

Brandt rested his chin in his hand and raised an eyebrow.

"What?" Kevin's eyes danced away.

"Let's see. We could talk about the weather…"

Kevin laughed, just the reaction he'd hoped for. Time to switch gears and see if he could uncover more of the boy's mysterious situation.

Trying to get the kid to talk was like peeling shrimp—slow and challenging––but worth the effort. "So I'm building a new center, and it's coming along really well. Pretty soon there'll be rooms."

"What? Like a motel?"

"Kind of. It's more like a sanctuary for people to come who don't feel safe anywhere else." Brandt smiled at him.

"I can't afford rent." Kevin chewed on his fingernail.

"It's free. There's a game room, a dining room, tutors, you name it." Brandt noticed the emphasis on I and not we.

Kevin's eyebrows shot halfway up his forehead. "Free? Why let people stay there for free?"

"Because I can. Because when I was your age, I ended up on the streets, in foster homes. I wish I'd had a safe place to go with a clean bed, hot shower, and some food." He shrugged, mirroring Kevin's favorite gesture.

The boy shook his head. "Yeah, but if I did, they'll say I ran away, and then they'll make me go to prison, and I'll have to work on the chain gang."

"Prison? The chain gang? How old are you? Nine?"

Kevin nodded, his eyes wide as plates.

"You won't go to prison, I promise. And I'm pretty sure chain gangs are only in the movies." Brandt gritted his teeth and cursed whoever was filling the boy's head with lies. Although from his own stint in juvie, he knew it wasn't a stretch to call it jail.

The waitress delivered their shakes, and they slurped down the frosty beverages. How could he broach the topic of Kevin's living situation and parents?

Damn it, he'd just ask and hope for the best. "Who do you live with, Kevin?"

The boy stopped mid-gulp of his milkshake and gazed up with his puppy eyes. "My mom."

"Um, does she know you aren't in school today?" He was gaining Kevin's trust and didn't want to scare him off, but he also wanted him to be safe.

"No. She isn't around…" He resumed chewing on his ragged fingernail.

"Where is she? You can trust me. I can help."

"Why?" Kevin met his gaze again.

"Like I said, I came from a…tough situation." He really couldn't say hell, could he? Because it had been hell. "It took me time on the streets and on my own before I was able to escape, and if I can help you and other kids avoid that, then that's what I am here to do."

He stared at Kevin, willing him to accept the help, to not be too scared to accept it.

Kevin kept his eyes glued to his milkshake. "I like it better when she's gone. Hate it when she brings home the guys. They're mean. I try to get out or hide. Later she's all upset, and if I'm around, she'll hit me with the spatula."

"What about your dad?" *Shit.*

Kevin shrugged but didn't reply.

"Is your dad around?" Brandt kept his tone calm and steady.

"Don't have one. My mom said the dirty bastard took off when I was a baby." Kevin's voice remained matter of fact.

"So you never knew your dad?"

Kevin shook his head. "No."

"Well, both my parents were around for a while, and I can tell you I wish I'd never known mine. Either of them." His fingers curled around his now-empty milkshake.

Kevin lifted his big brown eyes. "But look at you. You're rich. You surf in the middle of the day. You did all right."

Brandt's chest tightened. On the surface, he'd turned out okay. Despite the horrific nightmare of his childhood. Or lack of childhood. If Kevin saw him as a beacon of hope, it was a good thing, right? Something made him want to live up to the boy's expectations.

Although he hadn't acted like a good guy with Alyssa

when he'd run out. He'd acted like a prick, and he needed to fix it.

"You'll do all right too." He'd make sure of it.

The waitress plunked down two giant platters overflowing with French fries and massive cheeseburgers and they both dug in. The discussion was done for now.

When it came time to take Kevin home, he refused to share an address. Brandt had no choice but to drop him off at the beach. He made sure Kevin still had his business card. What else could he do at this point?

Time to fix things––at least to fix things with Alyssa. He steered the car to Tearmann House.

AFTER PARKING next to Alyssa's car, Brandt hesitated, because as much as he'd tried to forget the visual of her mussed and soft the other morning, he couldn't.

He'd tried to pigeonhole the memories and make sense of all of it the last few days, but he hadn't been able to focus on work. When he'd managed to catch a few hours of sleep, she'd invaded his dreams. No woman had distracted him this way. Ever.

Damn it, he cared about her. Always had. And he'd panicked. Screwed up. They needed to clear the air before Nick returned. If they didn't get the situation under control, Nick would suspect in a heartbeat. And he couldn't jeopardize their friendship. Although technically, he'd done exactly that.

And he still had no clue what to do. Much less how to discuss it. Usually, the women he chose knew the score— casual, no strings, no expectations. He didn't lie. He made it clear commitment wasn't for him.

Of course, if he were honest with himself, he wanted to

lock Alyssa in the bedroom with him for the next ten days. Lose himself in their amazing connection. Much as he'd love to spend the next few weeks with her, he couldn't risk it. No way in hell could he maintain the emotional distance he had with every other woman. Alyssa was different. Special. And off limits. At least, from now on.

Because maintaining his distance from her was the only way he could ensure his shitty gene pool didn't rear its ugly head. He couldn't risk potentially harming Alyssa one day.

Time to try to make her see reason. Again. He smacked his hand on the steering wheel--because that plan went so well the first time when they'd ended up in bed. Well, taking the long route via the couch and then the floor. He sucked in a deep breath.

Although he'd just eaten, he'd suggest going to lunch. Talking in a public restaurant would be much safer because he couldn't rip her clothes off. He strode into his building and paused in the conference room doorway. His breath caught in his throat. Because the last time she'd been alone at the enormous table, she'd come apart in his arms for the first time. *Fuck.*

"Alyssa." Brandt paused in the doorway.

"I'm on my way out. Nice of you to show up." Her face was paler than usual, her stormy blue eyes hard.

He lifted a hand. "I'm sorry. Look, can I take you to lunch? Talk?"

She rolled her eyes and gripped her honey-colored satchel close to her side.

"Lunch, Alyssa?" Would she give him a chance to explain? To apologize?

She waved one slender hand. "Fine. Only if you're planning on serving up an explanation."

"We'll talk and I'll do my best, okay? Laguna Coffee Co. work for you?" Laguna Coffee Co. didn't include table service. Because ensuring no waiter or waitress eavesdropping on what promised to be a very interesting conversation was important.

"Sure, I need some air and we can sit outside." She sauntered past him toward the door. A hint of her citrusy fragrance wafted to him, and he sucked in a breath. Now he knew how she tasted, the scent of her was even more tempting. He held his breath––time to get a grip.

On the walk to the restaurant, Brandt struggled not to stare at her endless legs showcased in a pencil skirt and stilettos. *Focus, man. Stay calm.* His stomach coiled into ropes.

When they joined the long order line at the restaurant, he maintained arm's distance. Safer that way. They ordered, took their number to a small outdoor table, and he scooted his chair to the farthest point away from her.

"So how have you been?" *Lame.* Was that the best he could come up with? He cleared his throat. "Sorry. I'm really sorry I left the way I did yesterday. It's not you. It's me."

Alyssa choked on her iced tea. "You aren't giving me 'the it's not you, it's me.' Seriously, Brandt?"

If that old cliché, looks could kill, were accurate he'd be burned at the stake. He massaged the two-day scruff on his jaw, finding comfort in the roughness beneath his palm.

"Let me try again. Look, Alyssa, you know I've always cared about you." *Shit.*

"Cared about me. Like you care about Bailey or maybe care about the score of the football game? This was a mistake." She rose and reached for her purse.

"Wait." He caught her wrist, determined to halt her progress. "Please, this isn't easy."

Without a word, she sank back into her chair, her purse gripped in both hands. His heart tugged in his chest. Damn, she was so gorgeous.

"Look, I'm sorry I left the way I did. I didn't plan on it,

hell, didn't plan on any of this. You deserve better...You deserve the best, which sure as hell isn't me."

Her eyes narrowed. "Yes, I definitely do. So, what's the deal?"

"I panicked, okay? I thought of Nick feeding me to the sharks and just had to—I don't know—just had to get some distance." Sweat popped up on the back of his neck.

She shifted forward, covering his forearm with her cool hand. "Nick's my brother. But he doesn't dictate who I see and what I do. My decision. I know it might be a little awkward with you guys being best friends, but it's not like we're in high school. I mean, we're all adults, right?"

The feel of her smooth palm against his skin sent sparks flaming through him and instantly, he was hard. He shifted out of reach. This was ridiculous. If she touched him again, he'd lose control.

Right now? All he wanted to do was toss her over his shoulder and carry her to his car. Damn her brother. "Yeah, but Nick isn't just my best friend, he's my family."

"Are you planning on screwing me over? Hurting me? Using me?" She arched a perfectly groomed eyebrow.

"Of course not." She was complicated. Special. Irresistible. And he could never be worthy of her.

"So what's the problem? We're in this with open eyes, right?" Her rosy lips curved upward.

She had an answer for everything. "You're not listening to me..."

"Because I don't see why we need to deny ourselves over the next few weeks. Why fight it? Can't we have this amazing physical relationship now and remain friends after?" She reached for his hand. This time he didn't pull away. Couldn't release their connection.

Damn. Was it possible? If she could do it, he could too. Right? He was strong. He could do this. He'd escaped hell as a child and built a business empire, so why couldn't he do this?

She massaged his hand with her long slender fingers, and his jeans grew uncomfortably tight. His brain emptied. He turned his hand over and intertwined his fingers with hers. Screw it, he'd never claimed to be a saint.

"Damn it, Alyssa. This is a terrible idea, but…let's go."

Lunch forgotten; he tugged her to her feet. He needed her now.

They half-ran/half-walked back to the office parking lot and dove into his car. He peeled out, intent solely on getting to his house. If Nick killed him, at least he'd die a happy man, right?

CHAPTER 10

Alyssa's eyes popped open, the sound of her stomach rumbling rousing her out of a light doze. Brandt was propped on a sinewy forearm, smiling down at her, his cobalt eyes heavy-lidded. Her breath caught. "Please tell me my stomach didn't wake you up."

He laughed and rubbed her protesting belly. "Sounds like an angry bear in there. I cheated you out of lunch, didn't I?"

Her lips twitched. "Now that you mention it…"

"I'm pretty sure I've got half a pizza in the fridge. That's a start."

He rose and tugged her to her feet.

"Hold on. I need some clothes." Heat flooded her cheeks. Sure, she wasn't an insecure teenager anymore, but she wasn't stroll-around-in-her-birthday-suit confident either. Especially since he was perfect with his chiseled pecs, incredible abs, and smooth tanned skin.

"I think those didn't make it upstairs." He winked. "Don't start being shy now. You look incredible."

"Come on. Give me a T-shirt and some boxers. You need

to put something on too, or we may not make it all the way to the kitchen."

"Fine." He grumbled and strode to his dresser and pulled out a couple of T-shirts and two pairs of patterned boxer shorts.

She cringed when she looked down at the baggy shorts that hung to her knees. So much for her brief stint as a seductress. Of course, he looked like an underwear model from a Hollywood billboard.

"Remember I know exactly what's under those clothes." He winked.

He clasped her hand and led her downstairs. The floor-to-ceiling windows, pale cream walls, and teak-colored wood were stunning. Paintings of seascapes dotted the walls, vivid scenes of white-capped oceans and sharp slashing cliffs. Nothing muted or pastel— dramatic and stark images dominated. Her interior designer heart approved.

When they reached the kitchen, Brandt yanked open the stainless-steel refrigerator and pulled out a huge cardboard to-go box from her favorite pizza place. Sliding it onto the charcoal-gray granite countertop, he popped the lid and gobbled down half a piece in one bite.

"Oh, sorry. Do you want me to heat it up for you?" he mumbled between mouthfuls.

She smiled as he inhaled it before she could even pick up a slice. "Glad to see I'm not the only hungry one. And don't bother, pizza's the one food I can eat without reheating."

"I need to get back to Tearmann House at some point today." She bit into the wood-fired perfection. Go figure-- her appetite had miraculously reappeared. Just anxiety related, not eating disorder related. Phew.

He leaned forward and wiped a crumb from the corner of her lip. "Me too. I'll drive us back."

Her skin tingled from the brush of his fingers. When he

paused, simply staring into her eyes, she turned and kissed his broad square palm, keeping her gaze locked with his. Instantly, his pupils flared, and heat bloomed low in her belly. *Down, girl.*

Work. Career. Priorities.

She retreated a step, away from the dangerous distraction of his hands. If he touched her again, her brain would turn off. "I thought you wanted the center done as soon as possible. Aren't we on a deadline?"

"Tearmann's mine and I am your boss, right? I don't think it's civilized to skip dessert, do you?" His grin was devilish as he advanced toward her.

She stepped out of reach, giggling at his newly revealed mischievous side. "Brandt—"

"Resistance is futile." He scooped her up and tossed her over one broad shoulder, firefighter style.

"Put me down," she managed through peals of laughter. She smacked his fine butt. Why not? It was right there in front of her in all its round muscular perfection.

"With pleasure." He deposited her on the couch and landed on top of her, nestling his narrow hips between her thighs.

Anticipation surged through her system, and the last bubble of laughter evaporated when he nibbled on her earlobe.

"Mmm, this spot is especially sweet." His lips traveled down the side of her sensitive neck, goosebumps erupting along her skin.

She arched against him, eager for his mouth on hers, eager for more. Plunging her fingers into his thick dark hair, she couldn't help but beg. "Kiss me."

He complied, slanting his mouth across hers. Their tongues tangled and swirled, and he tasted like the hint of pizza and something uniquely Brandt.

Who was she kidding? She could spend the rest of her life in his embrace, so what was another hour? Wasn't this what she'd been after?

They could always work late, right?

~

BRANDT SMILED as he drove to Alyssa's condo, eager at the prospect of taking her on a real date. The more time he spent with Alyssa, the more time he wanted to spend with Alyssa. A first for him.

Over the last week, they'd fallen into a pattern of working together during the day and spending the night with each other. Being with her had become natural, like breathing.

Each day, he learned a little more about her. He'd always known she was funny but hadn't realized how dry and sarcastic her sense of humor was. He'd never laughed so much and eagerly awaited each new witty observation to tumble from her lips. He'd never found humor to be sexy, but with Alyssa, it ratcheted up his libido.

Each time they slept together, unfamiliar sensations of protectiveness and tenderness flooded his chest. Each day, he found it more difficult to tamp down his unfamiliar feelings. He smacked his palm onto the steering wheel. Damn it.

He gripped the SUV's steering wheel. Sweat prickled on his brow, and his shoulders tensed. He shook his head. Nick would return in less than forty-eight hours. They were living on borrowed time.

Because she'd move on and marry a guy who was worthy of her, a man who would give her the family she wanted. The family she deserved.

To protect her, he had no choice but to leave her. His scars ran deep. Who knew if the violence his parents had embodied lurked beneath the surface waiting to erupt in a moment of anger? He'd never survive if he hurt her. And there was Nick, the closest thing to family he'd ever had. He'd lose them both.

But damn it, she deserved to be wined and dined and pampered. He'd make tonight special. A memory he could savor for years to come.

He'd finagled last-minute front-row tickets to the Pageant of the Masters. Sometimes having business connections paid off. Usually, Laguna's Festival of Arts' magical production was sold out a year in advance. People traveled from around the world to see the unique show during its seven-week run. Over the course of an hour and a half, models posed to recreate classical and contemporary works of art, or tableaux vivant.

He parked in front of Alyssa's condo, and she opened the front door before he could exit the car. Like a slow-motion reel, she sauntered toward him on mile-long bronzed legs shown off by a short black skirt, her golden hair cascading around her shoulders. His throat tightened and his jaw dropped.

"Hi, handsome." She whipped open the passenger door and slid inside before he had the chance to shut his mouth.

When she leaned in to give him a kiss, he clasped her head in his hands and savored her delicious mouth. Something shifted in his chest. *Compartmentalize.*

"Ready for a great night?" He shifted away, struggling to tamp down the bands constricting his chest. Was it possible someone could smell like sunshine?

"I can't wait. I haven't been to the Pageant of the Masters in years, not since my parents were alive. My parents took Nick and me every summer. It's just too special to share with just anyone." She angled her head toward him. "It used to be one of my favorite family outings."

He reached for her hand and squeezed it. "I get it. I've

always gone alone but I wanted to go with you. I'm glad you're with me." At least for now.

"Me too." Her long slender fingers intertwined with his. She settled back into the plush leather seat and crossed one tantalizing tanned thigh across the other.

She met his gaze with a tentative smile. "Did you get us good seats?"

"Only front-row center. Only the best for you, beautiful." He injected some humor into his voice, anything to erase the shadows dimming her blue eyes. He swallowed again and forced his eyes back onto the road.

After a quick drive out to Laguna Canyon, he pulled into the festival's VIP parking lot. He grabbed the small cooler he'd stocked with champagne, strawberries, cheese, and crackers from the trunk.

A light breeze, characteristic of Orange County, lifted her hair away from her gorgeous face as they headed into the amphitheater. Voices buzzed with excitement around them, anticipation for the spectacle to come at a fever pitch. An usher directed them toward the front row.

So far, so good.

"Brandt Alyssa, hey." A husky male voice interrupted their progress.

They both stiffened. Oh shit. Christian Wolfe, one of his best friends and the owner of Vines Wine Bar. He was also buddies with Nick.

"Christian. Great to see you." Alyssa stepped forward and hugged him.

"Good to see you too. Are Nick and Sophie with you?" Christian glanced between them.

"No, they're still—" Alyssa began.

"Why do you—" Brandt said.

They laughed, and Brandt moved a step away from Alyssa. Christian couldn't suspect that he and Alyssa were spending more time naked than at work. Figured he'd run into someone connected with Nick. Laguna was too small of a town, damn it.

"Nick asked me to babysit. I mean, take care of Alyssa while he was gone, and so here we are." Brandt shrugged a shoulder, struggling to appear nonchalant.

Alyssa's nostrils flared and she pursed her full lips. She had to realize Christian could blow their cover if he suspected they were here as anything other than friends.

"Babysit? I might need a babysitter tomorrow night," a curvy brunette piped up from Christian's side, her tone suggestive.

Christian had a date? The guy was a military vet and despite owning a wine bar was kind of a loner. Maybe he wasn't the only one with secrets.

Alyssa squeezed his arm, digging her fingernails deep. "Babysitter for hire. That's Brandt. He's great at his job. Isn't that right, big brother?"

"Haha, yeah, Nick says I'm like a surrogate big brother." He rubbed the tight muscles on the back of his neck.

Expression impassive, Christian stared until the silence became uncomfortable.

"Aren't you going to introduce us to your date? Or are you babysitting too?" Alyssa's laugh was forced, at least to his ears.

The woman stared at him like he was a snack. "No, we're old friends. I'm Liz. Where are you guys sitting? Maybe we can all hang out together?"

"Oh, Brandt got us front-row seats. Isn't that sweet of him?" Alyssa squeezed his bicep again and burrowed her nails a little deeper. He sucked in a deep breath.

"Too rich for my blood." Christian shrugged. "We'll be back at Vines tonight around ten if you feel like coming by for a drink."

"Ten might be past my bedtime, right, Manny Brandt?" Alyssa patted his shoulder.

Christian barked out a laugh. "Manny? That's great. I'm going to remember that nickname."

"Haha, you're a riot." Brandt pried her hand off his arm. "Forget the nickname, dude. Nice meeting you, Liz."

Just a couple of friends attending a show. Keep telling yourself that, man. Talk about a reality check. They turned and headed down toward the front of the amphitheater in silence. Because seeing Christian was a reminder that their being together was a secret and had to remain a secret. Damn it, so much for enjoying a special date together.

When they reached their seats, he whipped out a velvety-soft green blanket from the top of the cooler to cover their legs. Although it was summer, once the sun set in Laguna, the ocean breeze kept it cool.

"Are we going to talk about what just happened?"

Without replying, he pulled out the bottle and two plastic flutes. "Champagne?"

"Why not?" Smiling, she accepted a faux-crystal flute.

"Look, you know we had to act like that in front of Christian. Remember this is our secret—your words. Imagine if Nick found out from someone else?"

"I guess you're right." She nodded.

"Can we put it behind us and focus on tonight? I really wanted this to be a special night for us." He reached for her bare thigh underneath the blanket and squeezed reassuringly.

"Me too."

The lights dimmed, the curtain lifted, and the performance began. He sighed and settled in close to her, cloaked in the protection of the starry night.

CHAPTER 11

When Brandt knocked on Alyssa's door, she leaned against the doorjamb and flashed him a mischievous grin. He held up a carryout bag containing their delicious Thai food dinner in one hand and the latest file of plans for the center in the other.

"Hi there, delivery boy. Do you have something for me?" She waggled her eyebrows, basking in the hot gleam in his eyes.

"Oh, I've got something for you all right." He growled, dropping the food bag and file to the floor, and grabbed her. He yanked her against him and there was his seemingly ever-present hard-on. Game on.

She wrapped her arms around him and laughed as she pressed her mouth to his. "You're insatiable."

"Are you complaining?" he murmured against her lips. He hurried them through the door and kicked it shut behind him.

Without interrupting their kiss, he swept her up in his arms, and she wound her legs around his waist. He strode into the bedroom and tossed her down onto the soft bed.

She laughed as she propped herself up onto her elbows, scooting away from him. He dove onto the bed, pinned her beneath him, and captured her mouth once again. Could she ever get enough of him?

Their clothes went flying and she lost herself in his hot hard body. Fast and furious, they rose and fell together in perfect sync. She cried his name as she came apart, and with a jerk and a groan, he flew over the edge with her.

She struggled to catch her breath, unable to move. Loving the heaviness of him on top of her. His beachy scent enveloped her--he truly smelled like the beach on a sunny day.

"You're smothering me, and I'm starving," she whispered into his ear and smacked him on his butt.

He nuzzled her neck and with one final kiss, rolled off her and pulled her to her feet. "Do you want me to heat up dinner, or are you fine with eating cold Pad Thai?"

Without waiting for an answer, he strode naked into the living room, looking around for the take-out bag.

"If the food is still there because I'm pretty sure you dropped the bag outside." She laughed and followed him.

He cracked the door open and snaked his arm out to grab their meal and the work file. Then he plucked his jeans off the floor, a casualty of their quick trip to the bedroom. He tugged the faded denim on, leaving the top button open, his ripped abs and those V's on full display.

Alyssa admired his muscular back and cute butt before she whipped a sweatshirt over her head and bundled her hair up into a topknot. "Let's heat it up. I'm not a fan of cold noodles." The food had to be icy after their detour into the bedroom.

"I know you like it hot, baby." He winked over his shoulder back at her.

Her heart warmed at his teasing. After almost two weeks

together, their passion showed no sign of diminishing. On the contrary, the more time they spent together, the more voracious her appetite for him grew.

As they became more familiar with each other's bodies and turn-ons, the sex grew more intense. More intimate. Beyond any of her schoolgirl fantasies.

And it wasn't just their bodies getting closer. When Brandt's guard came down, he'd flash a boyish grin or laugh without reserve. Who knew he'd have this lighter, sweeter side? Or that he could talk for hours? His vulnerability endeared him to her. In fact, her love deepened with each passing day.

He'd ripped open one of the containers and shoveled noodles into his mouth with a pair of chopsticks. His cheeks were puffed out like a chipmunk's. So much for heating up the food.

"Hungry?" She couldn't resist teasing him. She was extremely familiar with his unquenchable appetite.

He glanced up, a dark brow quirked, a wicked gleam lighting his blue eyes. "I need some fuel right now, but I'm sure I can find some energy to gobble you up in about twenty minutes."

Goosebumps prickled along her skin, and her cheeks heated. Smiling at him, she went over to the cabinet to pull down a plate and a couple of wineglasses. Her heart sang. Could she be any happier?

"Fuel, it is. Chardonnay or sauvignon blanc?"

He waved a hand, his mouth still stuffed.

She microwaved the other container and opened a bottle of chardonnay. When the bell dinged, they moved to the kitchen island and settled down with dinner. They ate in companionable silence for a few minutes, both focused on the delicious meal.

Once her stomach quieted down, she took a cleansing

breath. Nerves fluttered in her belly, but she needed a game plan. They needed a game plan. Would they tell Nick and Sophie tomorrow?

Why not?

"So I'm picking up the honeymooners tomorrow. Do you want to come with me to the airport?" Her heart accelerated to a gallop.

Brandt's relaxed expression froze, and he dropped his gaze to the food. He placed his fork onto his plate and shifted back in his chair. He didn't say a word.

"Brandt?" Her stomach twisted. His icy mask hadn't been on display since the night of the wedding.

He shoved away from the island and stalked to the window, his back rigid. Sliding his hands into the pockets of his jeans, he angled back toward her. His eyes were freezing chips of aqua glass.

He leveled his gaze on hers. Finally. "I was trying to enjoy tonight. Forget that this was our last night together…"

"Our last night? Are you serious?" Her pulse thrummed in her temples.

He inclined his head. "Nick returns tomorrow, so yeah, our last night."

"Are you kidding me right now?" Irritation flickered through her.

He folded his arms across his bare chest. "You're the one who created this plan. Two weeks—two weeks to get each other out of our systems. Why do you think anything's changed?"

She flinched. His words a slap to her face. "Nothing's changed?"

He shook his head.

She clenched her hand into a fist around the stem of the wineglass, willing it not to shatter. Willing her heart not to shatter.

"Everything's changed. How can you stand there and pretend this has just been sex? We've been happy. We've been a couple. We've spent every minute together, and now you say nothing's changed?" Fury licked down her spine.

He pivoted back toward the window, his broad shoulders hunched. Unable to face her, the coward. "Look, I'm sorry. It's better this way. I told you I can never be the man you need. And yeah, we had a great time. But we agreed on two weeks." He continued to stare out the window.

"You jerk." She lobbed the wineglass at his head, wincing as it smashed against the window frame about an inch from his right ear. Couldn't she even do that right? Couldn't she hit his big hard head?

He turned now, sidestepped the broken glass, and started toward her. "Be reasonable. We can figure this out. I can't risk my friendship with Nick. He'd kill me if he ever found out. Hell, he'd probably kill you too. Think about it—"

"Get away from me. How can you be so cold? What are you made of?" She backed away from him. If he touched her, she'd collapse. He needed to leave her apartment before she lost it. Now.

Something flickered behind his eyes. "Alyssa…"

"Get out." The pounding at her temples intensified into an excruciating tempo.

"Look, we can talk this out…" He stepped closer.

"Get out. I don't want to talk to you. And don't show up at Tearmann tomorrow either. I don't want to see you." She pointed at him. Willed her body not to betray her. She refused to cry in front of him. No way in hell would he see how he was breaking her heart.

He hesitated, opened his mouth.

"I'm serious. Go. Leave Bailey here." She braced herself against the counter and clung to it with her hands because her wobbly legs threatened to fail her. If he didn't leave soon, she'd lose it.

"I'm sorry." His gaze locked with hers for a brief second, and then he pivoted and left the room.

Alyssa remained rooted to the spot, her limbs paralyzed, and her mind frozen. Subtle sounds of him gathering his things and the quiet click of the door closing sounded final.

Her knees buckled, betraying her, and she sank to the floor. Bailey bounded over to snuggle with her. She wrapped her arms around the giant dog and buried her face in her velvety fur.

Sobs wracked her body as her heart splintered in her chest. Had that scene really just happened? He'd morphed into another person. A taciturn stranger. Not the man who'd saved her from bullies when she was a troubled teenager. The man who soothed her and made her feel like an elegant swan, not the ugly duckling she was. The man who agreed not to tell her overprotective big brother about the incident.

Definitely not the man who'd fulfilled her teenage infatuation by being her constant companion, her exciting lover, her best friend over the last few weeks.

Was she delusional to believe things had changed? Didn't actions speak louder than words? He'd been a caring, attentive lover. Considerate. Kind. Passionate.

But his actions tonight showed a totally different man altogether. A man who didn't love her. Didn't want her. At least didn't want her enough to tell Nick.

CHAPTER 12

$\mathcal{A}$lyssa zipped around an ancient minivan that'd apparently decided to drop off its passengers in the middle lane of traffic at John Wayne Airport instead of bothering to pull up to the curb. With a sharp turn, she screeched delicately into the appropriate lane to pick up the returning honeymooners.

Satisfied with her position, she flipped down the visor to double-check that her careful arsenal of mirrored aviator sunglasses, half a bottle of industrial-strength eye drops, and one pound of under-eye concealer camouflaged her sleepless night. If she could get Nick and Sophie talking about their experiences in the South of France, she could hopefully just nod and smile and focus on the road. Shouldn't be too tough. Sophie adored France, and as a newly minted writer, she had a natural talent for spinning an engaging tale.

No way could Alyssa risk a detailed discussion of the last two weeks until she'd fortified her defenses. Her plan was simple—drop them off at their home and use work as an excuse to put some distance between them. Because Nick knew her too well, and she'd never been able to lie to him. At least since her high school "difficult period."

And she couldn't wait to hear about the honeymoon. She was overjoyed for Nick and Sophie's happiness, especially since both of them had been wounded when they'd met. Despite Nick's fear of intimacy, Sophie's love had opened her brother's heart for the first time since their parents died. They were perfect together.

She massaged the hollow under her breastbone. Why couldn't she find true love? Why couldn't Brandt be the one for her? Was it really just about Nick's friendship, or did his scars run deeper? And would her stubborn brother ever approve of anyone she dated?

She squeezed her eyes shut. Indulged again in the beautiful, foolish movie she'd fashioned in her heart: She and Brandt living together in his house with a soccer team of children and their own dog, no longer needing to borrow Bailey. A loud, boisterous, loving family filling his now-empty house, a place where the children never felt lonely or lost.

She flipped the visor down again. Slid her sunglasses down and stared into her own bloodshot eyes. "Wake up, Alyssa Morgan. You. Are. Alone. Brandt doesn't want to try."

A tap on the passenger window jolted her. Sophie was waving. Alyssa shoved her glasses back on her nose and fumbled with the door handle while Sophie ran around to the driver's side.

She managed to open the door, stepped out, and embraced her new sister-in-law. She squeezed Sophie and smiled at her brother over her shoulder. Her heart warmed at his relaxed expression and genuine grin.

"The parking police here are insane. Let me pop the trunk." Where Nick couldn't dissect her expressions or appearance.

"Let's get the bags in the car, and we'll fill you in on the way back to Laguna," Nick said. He loaded the suitcases into the trunk, and they jumped into the car.

Alyssa eased away from the curb and headed toward the highway. "So how was it? I want to hear every detail. Well, not *every* detail."

Sophie clapped her hands together and described the picturesque beaches in Antibes, the delicious wines of Provence, and the world-famous restaurant at the Hotel Belles Rives, F. Scott and Zelda Fitzgerald's former residence. Alyssa was happy to keep them on topic.

"So what about you? What's new over the last few weeks?" her brother asked from the back seat.

Alyssa kept her eyes glued on the road. She crossed the toes on her left foot. "New? Nothing really… Just working a lot on Tearmann House."

"How's it coming along?"

"Great. Scott's a good project manager, and you did an amazing job with the design, Nick. I feel really lucky being part of it all."

"What about Brandt?"

"Brandt? What about Brandt?" Her voice rose an octave, and she sucked in a huge breath.

Nick's voice grew curious. "Well, it's his center, right? Has he been hands-on?"

"Hands-on?" A bubble of hysteria rose in her throat. If her brother had any idea exactly where Brandt's hands had been.

"Alyssa, what's up with you? Why are you repeating everything I'm saying?"

Sophie's gaze burned into her. So much for playing it cool.

"Sorry, sorry. I just didn't get much sleep last night." Understatement of the century. Where was their exit?

"Oooh, is there a hot new guy in the picture?" Sophie shifted in her seat to focus on Alyssa.

"New guy?" Nick leaned forward and wrapped his hand around the edge of Alyssa's seat.

"Stop it, you two. There's no new guy." Technically not a lie. "The center is going great. Brandt's been there a fair amount, at least until the other day." *When he broke my heart.*

"The other day? He didn't take off, did he?" Impatience threaded through Nick's voice.

"Take off?"

Nick threw a hand in the air. "Alyssa, what is going on with you? Is Brandt in town, or did he go off somewhere?"

"I don't know." Finally, the complete truth.

"Why wouldn't he tell you if he weren't coming in? Are you two fighting again? Hell, I asked him to look out for you…" Nick flopped back into his seat.

"Oh yeah, I almost forgot. What is wrong with you? You embarrassed me." If she weren't driving, she'd grab him by the ear and twist it the way her mother had when they were kids.

He plucked a piece of lint off his pants and glanced out the window.

"Nick! You asked Brandt to babysit Alyssa? Seriously?" Sophie turned in her seat to look at him.

"Not babysit, just keep an eye on." He held up his hands as if to ward off both his sister's and his wife's glares. "Look, I'm sorry, but you're alone. I just wanted him to be a surrogate big brother…"

Alyssa's foot stomped involuntarily, jerking all of them in their seats. Not great to brake while flying at seventy-five mph down the busy highway.

"She's not in high school, Nick. Has he been this way since you guys were kids?" Sophie's voice grew sympathetic, even as she braced her hand against the dashboard.

"He's always been this way. A royal pain in the butt. When will you realize I'm grown up and will date whoever I want?" Alyssa's stomach clenched.

He leaned forward again. "Who are you dating?"

Sophie swatted his hand. "Nick. Stop it."

"Can you two have kids soon so he has somebody else to be mother hen for?" Her and Brandt's relationship was their secret. Nick needed to drop it.

"One step at a time, my friend." Sophie smiled.

Thank goodness Sophie was there as a buffer now. For a few blessed minutes, they drove along in comfortable silence.

Their exit loomed ahead, and Alyssa swallowed to relieve her parched throat. She headed into Laguna and as they cruised closer to the Pacific, the knots in her belly loosened. The powerful beauty of Mother Ocean never failed to soothe her. She could handle this.

"Once I drop off our stuff, I'll cruise down to Tearmann House. I'll call Brandt so we can all get together and review what's happened so far, what's next." Nick piped up from the back seat.

"Don't you guys need to rest? Aren't you exhausted from your trip? And your part of this is done for right now. No need for you to come by." The words poured out like an overflowing faucet. So much for discretion.

Nick huffed out an irritated breath. "What is up with you? You're acting really weird. What's wrong?"

"Nothing, nothing's wrong. I just…I just want to work on Tearmann House a little more before you see it and judge what I'm doing." She bit her lip to avoid screaming a resounding no. No way was Nick coming to the center today. Although she'd ordered Brandt not to come in, he didn't exactly excel at listening to her requests, did he?

"Judge? You know I think you do an incredible job. We've always talked about me being hands-on through the end.

This project is just as much mine as yours and Brandt's." He injected a note of hurt into his voice.

A twinge of guilt surged through her. "Sorry, just too much caffeine this morning. Of course, if you're up for coming in, I'd love for you to see the progress."

Alyssa sighed in gratitude when she pulled into the driveway and parked in front of their house.

While Nick unloaded the bags, Sophie came around to the driver's side of the car and hugged her again. She tilted her head. "Are you sure you're okay?"

Once again Alyssa was thankful for her mirrored sunglasses. Sophie was perceptive and caring, and she already felt like a sister. They'd grown close right off the bat. But Sophie was married to Nick, and she couldn't risk confiding in her about Brandt now.

Life felt complicated all of a sudden.

"Of course I'm fine. I'm just so glad you guys had an amazing trip and made it home safely. I can't wait to see all the pictures."

"Maybe we should have you and Brandt over tonight for dinner and look at the photos." Sophie turned to lean into Nick, who'd come up by her side and slid his arm around her.

"I really am tired and will probably crash right after work, but later this week, of course. Oh, and your fur babies are inside the house waiting for you guys."

Nick shifted away and pulled Alyssa in for a hug. Leaning back, he looked down at her, his brow now furrowed. "You feel really skinny. Are you sure…"

"I'm fine." She needed to escape. Pronto.

"You're eating?"

"I've been eating for years now, so please just stop. I think too much Mediterranean sun has fried your brain." She shoved him away.

"Fine, fine. I'll see you later today at Tearmann House."

Plastering a smile on her face, she slid into the front seat of her car and waved as she reversed away from them.

Narrow escape.

CHAPTER 13

Brandt stared out the window of the downtown San Francisco high-rise and took another swig of Macallan. When he'd bolted from Alyssa's house, getting out of town had seemed like a brilliant idea. Because there had been no way he could face Nick yet, especially after Alyssa assumed they'd pick them up and drop the bomb that they were a couple.

He slammed down his drink and paced around the vast penthouse suite. In the moment, all he had considered was putting some space between himself and Alyssa. Some space between Nick. All he'd had to do was call the airfield and schedule a pilot. He had a private plane at his disposal so why not use it for a semi-emergency?

A couple of days in San Francisco to catch up with some of his buddies in the tech world. Those guys knew him as the carefree genius who'd scored young with his Garda security program and always scored with the ladies. They'd remind him of how his life had to be.

Instead of having a blast with the guys, like he'd used to do, his brain kept flashing back to the devastation on

Alyssa's beautiful face, the shock in her stormy-sky eyes when he'd told her they were through. His chest constricted again.

So while his buddies were out at the latest trendy club, he'd retreated to the hotel to be alone. It wasn't like he was pleasant to be around. He returned to the table and poured another two fingers of whiskey.

Damn it, why was she so shocked? She'd been the one to promise two weeks with no strings, who'd encouraged him to compartmentalize.

And then she'd wanted to change the rules of the game she'd started? What did she expect?

Had she really thought they'd pick up Nick and Sophie at the airport and say, "Oh, by the way, we're a couple now—aren't you excited?"

He resumed his pacing.

When he'd gotten home, he'd flipped on the lights and looked around. His haven. His home. He'd always enjoyed it alone, but now Alyssa appeared everywhere.

A vase of red gerbera daisies on the living room table. A pale blue sweater lying across the armchair. He'd crossed to the chair and picked it up, sniffing the soft material that carried her citrusy scent, a reminder of her silky skin against his.

Damn, damn, damn it all to hell.

He'd pitched the sweater away from him, strode to the kitchen, popped open a dark lager, and downed a mouthful. He never should've allowed himself to succumb to temptation. To sink into the fantasy of Alyssa belonging to him. She was just way too damn perfect. Way too good for him. He wasn't worthy of her.

What had he been thinking? Nick had asked him to watch over Alyssa. To protect her. Instead, he'd allowed Alyssa in deeper than he'd ever imagined. Hell, he was crazy about her.

If he saw Nick now, he wouldn't be able to pretend indifference.

How could he face his best friend? He snorted again—Nick would go ballistic. He and Nick were like brothers, but Alyssa was off-limits.

If either of the Morgans had any concept of the true extent of his sordid past, not just a vague explanation about his abusive, addictive parents…

No, they'd both be disgusted by the full truth about the drugs, the thievery, the horrors he'd witnessed. He came from scum. Sure, he'd clawed and fought his way out of the gutter. He'd escaped and survived. Thrived even.

But blood didn't lie. He'd done Alyssa a favor. And now he'd pay for his selfish indulgence knowing he'd broken her heart. Although he'd destroyed his own in the process. Time to get royally wasted and forget. At least for a few hours.

A HORRIFIC BANGING sound jolted Brandt awake. What the hell? He sat up with a groan and looked around for the source of the noise drilling into his brain. His phone lay on the carpet beside the couch and was currently spewing the most godawful racket he'd ever heard.

He snatched it up and yeah, the day got worse, it was Nick. *Shit.* Just what he needed—an opportunity to lie to his best friend and feel guilty as hell. Maybe he should just let it go to voice mail.

No. He'd deal with this now despite the hammering in his skull and the queasiness in his gut. "Hey, you're back."

"Yeah, we got back this morning. Didn't Alyssa tell you she was picking us up?"

"Maybe, yeah. I'm up in San Francisco right now, so it

may have slipped my mind. How was France?" *Deflect, deflect, deflect.*

"It was awesome. You've got to check out Antibes. Amazing spot." Nick's voice warmed.

"One of these days. I'd like to hit Biarritz, though, to catch some waves." Surf was always a safe topic and the west coast of France boasted great surf, or so he'd heard.

"That would be killer. So how's Tearmann House? I couldn't get a straight answer out of Alyssa, and she was acting kind of weird. Were you able to keep an eye on her?"

Brandt threw one arm over his face and cleared his throat. How to answer like a protective friend instead of the guy who'd spent the last two weeks in bed with his best friend's little sister?

"You there?"

"Yeah, sorry, my head's killing me. Late night. Alyssa's doing a great job. She's really talented." And intelligent, and sweet, and is the most fascinating woman in the fucking universe.

"Yeah, she really is. But I'm concerned. Did you notice any new guy coming around or something?"

A wave of nausea hit him, and he took a steadying breath. "New guy?"

"Yeah, remember the reason I told you I wanted you to keep an eye on her is because she's had some really random dates from those dating apps. I want to make sure no asshole is hassling her or anything."

Brandt choked, every grain of sand in Death Valley now clogging his throat and lungs. Yeah, he was the asshole.

He ground his back teeth together—maybe they'd crumble into dust and join the pyramid of sand in his throat. "Dude, I saw her at work. Nobody is stalking her. Remember she's an adult and can take care of herself. She's fine."

"Okay, okay. Something's off, though, and if I have to kill some jerk for her, I will."

"Right." Could they change the subject anytime soon? Because if he'd had a sliver of doubt that Nick would kill him over Alyssa, now he had confirmation.

Nick grunted. "Why are you in San Francisco? I thought you were watching my dog."

"Oh, one of my college buddies invited me up last minute, and I figured why not? Alyssa took Bailey. Figured you'd be home today, and it wasn't a big deal. Remember, I don't have to answer to anyone, I can go where I want when I want." Was he actually babbling? And why did his heart ache?

Nick barked out a laugh. "You poor bastard. Keep telling yourself that. One of these days you'll meet someone who will change your mind and I'll remind you. Sophie's the best thing that ever happened to me. You'll see."

"Yeah, right. When hell freezes over." Brandt scoffed. He'd already met *the* woman. And Alyssa Morgan deserved better than him.

"When are you back? Let's the four of us have dinner and catch up. Do you think you and Alyssa can make nice for a few hours?"

"I'll be back tomorrow." If he didn't puke on the short flight home, it would be a miracle.

"Cool. Come over at seven."

Before Brandt could protest, Nick hung up. Dinner, it was. He flopped back onto the cushions and called the pilot. He was so screwed.

CHAPTER 14

*A*lyssa parked behind Brandt's vintage Corvette at Nick and Sophie's house. Apparently, he was back in town, although, of course, he hadn't bothered to get in touch with her. Jerk.

At least she'd had yesterday to focus on work without his distracting presence. She'd survived the day, jumping every time anyone arrived at Tearmann House. Wondering if it was Brandt. Deflated when it was Scott or one of the other contractors.

She'd avoided her brother when he'd stopped by the center, burying her nose in plans and shushing him when he tried to chat.

She'd worked late, forced herself to take a punishing run along the hills, and huffed through an intense yoga class followed by a restorative one guaranteed to "relax" her nerves. Despite her apartment seeming preternaturally quiet without Brandt's husky laugh and warm body, she'd eked out a few measly hours of sleep.

Unable to formulate an alibi without seeming suspicious, she'd accepted Nick and Sophie's dinner invitation.

Time to dig deep into her acting chops to play sister, friend, and nonchalant dinner guest. She grabbed the Caprese salad she'd thrown together and stepped out of the car.

Squaring her shoulders, she sauntered into the house. Laughter drifted toward her from the kitchen. Brandt's deep voice mingled with Sophie's. Oh, she'd missed his voice murmuring in her ear or making her laugh. Damn it.

"Here she is now. Red or white, Alyssa?" Sophie asked.

"I'd love to start with white. Do you have some chardonnay open?" Alyssa placed the salad onto the enormous granite kitchen island and hugged her sister-in-law.

Sophie dumped what looked like half the bottle into a wineglass and handed it to her with a wink. Did Sophie sense she needed some liquid courage?

She sipped, pleased with her self-restraint at not chugging it. *Don't look at him. Just don't look at him.* She waved one hand in his general direction. "Hey Brandt. Where's my brother?"

Sophie's lips curved upward. "Out on the deck manning the grill. We picked up some fresh Ahi steaks, good for you?"

"I love tuna. Anything I can do in here to help?" The hair on the back of her neck stood on end. Why wasn't Brandt outside with her brother?

"No, we kept it simple. I've got some Brussels sprouts roasting in the oven, so we're all set."

Dealing with Sophie was easy. And encountering Brandt first, even though she refused to look at him, helped. She needed a moment before seeing Brandt and Nick together. Because it would take a herculean effort to act casually. The other half bottle of wine couldn't hurt either.

"Brandt, will you go check on Nick? The veggies only need a few more minutes, so let him know he can sear the fish in the next few."

"Sure." He crossed to the French doors. Once he was gone, Alyssa's shoulders sagged. Round one over.

Sophie sliced up a fresh baguette and arranged it on a plate with a stoneware dish of softened butter. "Are you sure everything's okay? You look a little pale."

Alyssa plucked up a warm slice and nibbled on the crust, buying some time. Zack rubbed against her bare legs, and she reached down to stroke his silky fur.

"I'm fine. Just not sleeping very well. The animals missed you. Where's Bailey?"

"Bailey's outside, I think. If you need to talk—"

She polished off her bread and considered another piece. "I'm fine."

"Dinner." Nick bellowed from the deck.

"I see you haven't been able to teach him any manners yet." Their eyes met and they cracked up.

With a fortifying breath, Alyssa grabbed one of the dishes and followed Sophie out to the deck. Alyssa's heart softened at the candles and huge arrangement of sunflowers adorning the simple redwood picnic table. "The table looks gorgeous. Nice job getting flowers for your new wife."

"Oh, Brandt brought the flowers. Wasn't that thoughtful of him?" Sophie said.

Thoughtful was not the term she'd reserved for him. Not even in the top ten.

Figuring no response was expected, she set down the platter and hugged her brother as he transferred the fish from the grill to the platter.

"I put Brandt next to you so Nick and I can hold hands under the table like obnoxious honeymooners." Sophie's eyes shone as she grinned up at her husband.

Damn newlyweds. Alyssa struggled to keep her expression neutral as she placed her wineglass down and inched her place setting a little farther away from Brandt's. She slid onto the bench next to him, careful to avoid touching him. Awareness prickled along her skin. Would she burst into flames if she actually brushed against him?

Her casual words to Brandt taunted her. *Just compartmentalize.* Yeah, right. What had she been thinking? Present Alyssa cursed cavalier Past Alyssa. And now she was thinking of herself in the third person. Time to pull it together.

"Everything smells delicious. So give us some honeymoon stories, minus any of the sexy stuff." She sampled her seared ahi steak. If Nick suspected she wasn't eating, she'd never hear the end of it.

No extra tension needed tonight. Dealing with the handsome, aggravating man inches from her was all she could handle.

Brandt hadn't uttered a word since she and Sophie joined them outside. Glimpses of wavy, dark hair and tanned skin teased her peripheral vision. And she could smell his beachy, clean scent. His spine was rigid, and the hand not gripping his fork was fisted in his lap. *Good.* She hoped he was tied up in a million little knots. Just as she was.

"Oh, we'll show you guys the pictures after dinner and give you the illustrated version of the Morgans do France. Ha—that sounds funny." Sophie laughed as she leaned into Nick. He smiled and brushed his lips across her hair.

Alyssa's stomach tightened at the easy display of affection. She'd kill for Brandt to be able to act that way with her. Well, he had in private.

"It'll be better with the photos. Parts of the trip are kind of a blur." Nick waggled his eyebrows.

Alyssa had never seen her brother so relaxed. Happy. It warmed her heart, despite the niggling pinch of jealousy it evoked. If he could change this way, why couldn't Brandt?

Damn it. His feelings for her ran far deeper than a casual

fling. Actions spoke louder than words—well, all the other ones except for him running away.

Right now he was as still as a statue next to her. If only he didn't fear losing Nick. If she could just figure out how to help him overcome it. How could she get Nick and Brandt on the same page where she was concerned? Couldn't she get them to shift their perspective to a world where their being a couple made them all even closer? Like one big happy family?

When Nick and Sophie exchanged another scorching glance, the lightning bolt struck. Sophie. Sophie would help her. Because Nick wanted his best friend and his sister to find true love like he had. He just didn't recognize that they could find it with each other.

Warmed by the realization her friend could be her ally, she shifted gears. Brandt deserved a little bit of torture. She inched closer to him. His breath hissed out, he flinched and shifted away. He couldn't scoot further without tumbling off the end of the bench.

Encouraged by his visceral reaction, she slid her foot along his calf, savoring the feel of the crisp dark hair on his muscular leg. He slammed his glass down onto the picnic table, the wine sloshing over the rim.

"Dude, what's up?" Nick managed to drag his attention from Sophie. He quirked an eyebrow.

"Nothing, nothing. Sorry." Brandt shook his head and wiped up the spilled wine with his napkin.

Alyssa focused on her plate and innocently, she hoped, speared another morsel of fish. Brandt was crazy about her; she just had to convince him of it.

"Well, go ahead and fill us in on more details about Tearmann. Are you happy with how Alyssa's performing?" Nick asked.

Alyssa choked on a Brussels sprout and erupted into a

coughing fit when it went down the wrong pipe. Brandt thumped her back. Hard.

Heat seared her skin through the thin cotton of her blouse. She grabbed her wine and gulped it down, then dabbed her lips with her napkin. Coughing up half a lung was not the way to act nonchalant or seductive.

Brandt retreated to his half of the bench and paused before answering. "Sure, she definitely knows how to perform." His tone was neutral, his expression deadpan.

Alyssa squirmed and flicked her gaze to her brother. "Was there a question about me kicking ass and taking names?"

Nick downed a mouthful of wine. "Of course not. Why so prickly? I'm just trying to see if it's all on track. It seemed that way when I stopped by."

"I think I'm performing quite well. Right?" She smiled at Brandt and rubbed her foot against him again.

To his credit, he merely winced this time and drew his leg out of reach. "Everything is great. On schedule. Not sure what else you want to know." He shrugged.

The flush rising under his tan cheeks betrayed his discomfort. She was getting to him. Time to dial it up a notch. She reached across Brandt for another piece of bread and pressed her breasts against his arm. He sucked in his breath and held it.

Who knew torturing him could be so much more fun than ignoring him? She stifled a giggle as she shifted back into her seat.

Sophie stared owlishly from across the table. Her antenna apparently had detected something more than the usual tension between Brandt and Alyssa. Thankfully, her brother remained oblivious.

If only he'd remain oblivious to her choice of lover. Or at least open to his best friend and sister being a couple. Yes, she'd confide the bare minimum to Sophie, just enough to enlist her help.

Her love for Brandt. Her certainty he cared for her too. Maybe even loved her. His staunch refusal to get involved with her because of Nick. Nick was family to him, and he refused to jeopardize their bond. His conviction her brother would never approve of him. Or approve of anyone, really.

Although she certainly wouldn't share they'd been sleeping together, and Brandt had dumped her when they returned from France. If she disclosed their true relationship without Brandt's permission, they were doomed. No, although she trusted Sophie, she and Brandt's relationship was private, and she wouldn't betray his confidence. He'd never forgive her.

Besides, her friend was married to her brother. And married people told each other everything. Or so she'd heard.

Maybe Sophie could convince Nick his baby sister was no longer a child. Help clear the pathway with him so Brandt would feel comfortable moving forward. Show her brother that Brandt and Alyssa deserved the same kind of all-encompassing love he'd found.

To remind him love didn't have any rhyme or reason, that Cupid struck when you least expected it. Sometimes the arrow pierced two hearts with huge barriers blocking their union. Or one giant hurdle—her stubborn, overprotective big brother.

How could she get Nick to not only see reason but also give their relationship a fair chance? He'd been just as much a player as Brandt. Nick needed to overcome his own irrational caution where she was concerned and show Brandt the wall between them could be crossed.

Why did it have to be so complicated?

She'd caught the wedding bouquet fair and square, right?

~

IF ALYSSA DIDN'T STOP TEASING him soon, Brandt was going to explode. What the hell was she up to? From the minute she had sat next to him, he'd been hard as stone. Each time she brushed against him, rubbed her foot on his bare leg, or tossed her long fragrant hair, his jeans became another size smaller.

When she pressed her full breasts against his arm a second excruciating time, he growled. He gripped his legs and struggled to focus. Sophie's lips were moving, but all he discerned was buzzing.

"What?" He had no clue what she'd said. What anyone had said for the last agonizing minutes of exquisite torture.

Alyssa had the audacity to smirk at him. Smirk, damn it. "She asked when Tearmann would be ready to open."

"We don't have a date yet. As soon as humanly possible." He raked his fingers through his hair, giving it a tug to shift the blood flow from his lower half to his brain.

He couldn't keep up with Alyssa's moods. One minute she spit daggers at him, and the next she rubbed against him like a cat in heat. Dealing with her anger was easier. Why wasn't she angry? Especially after the way he'd rejected her again.

He fought to keep his breath even--he had self-control. Hell, he'd kept himself under control since he was nine years old. Until Alyssa had unleashed feelings he'd never experienced. Even if somehow Nick was cool with them being together, it was still impossible. Alyssa believed her brother's attitude was their sole obstacle. Not even close.

If Alyssa learned the truth, if she learned of the Mount Etna of roadblocks, she'd sprint in the opposite direction. He'd let her in closer than anyone before. But he couldn't tell her all of it. He'd gone to great lengths to bury the darkness from which he'd sprung.

No, he couldn't renege on the solemn promise he'd made to himself when he'd been shivering behind a dumpster. Biting his lip so hard it bled to keep from whimpering when he heard his father yelling his name. Knowing his father would whip him when he found him.

Both his parents had been addicts, always scrounging for the next fix. Never bothering with pesky things like feeding their only child or making sure he got to school.

He'd just been a nuisance to them, a creature hampering their good time. At least that's what his mother had always said. She wished he'd never been born because having him was just a drag. A burden.

When she'd beat the shit out of him with his father's belt, he wished he'd never been born either. While his bruises had healed, the emotional scars ran deep. Children of abusers become abusers. Children of addicts become addicts. He wasn't allowing anyone close enough to test out the theory.

So he'd vowed he'd never have kids. Never pass along the tainted genes he'd inherited.

Better to allow Alyssa to keep her illusions about him and maintain his relationship with his best friend. He never should have succumbed to temptation––yeah, he'd never recover from the best two weeks of his life. Tonight he'd descended into the ninth ring of hell.

"Brandt, are you okay? I asked if you'd go grab the gelato out of the freezer for us." Sophie said with raised brows.

"That's one hell of a hangover man. Never seen you so out of it." Nick pointed at him.

Shit. His trip down memory lane had lasted way too long but he'd claim the hangover as an excuse.

"Yeah, there was a lot of whiskey." He stood, eager for a brief respite from their speculation. "Four spoons?"

"For the third time, yes. Maybe don't have any more wine, though." Sophie grinned.

Time to shove the memories into the vault and time to cool off from the heat searing through him.

"Nick, why don't you go help Brandt. He seems confused." Alyssa's tone was sarcastic as hell.

Nick snickered. "Sure, why not. I'll make sure he doesn't crack another bottle of wine open."

Brandt gave him the middle finger and crossed the deck.

"You up for a surf in the morning? No waves in the Mediterranean and I didn't have a chance to go today."

Brandt rummaged through the freezer and grabbed the gelato without meeting Nick's gaze. "Sure, sounds great."

He managed to keep it together while they dished up dessert. All he had to do was hang on for another half an hour and he could escape.

When they returned to the table, Sophie and Alyssa's heads were huddled together and they were whispering. What the hell?

Sophie glanced up, then pointed at her placemat. "It took you long enough. You better not have been eating my portion. I'm still hungry."

"Don't worry. There's plenty of your favorite flavor." Nick set the salted caramel gelato on the table and settled in next to Sophie.

Brandt slid onto the bench, leaving as much space as possible without falling off. Alyssa scooped a huge spoonful, turned her head to provide him a more direct view, and took a long slow lick.

His breath hissed out. Alyssa was killing him. He inhaled his gelato--the sooner he finished, the sooner he could escape her torture.

CHAPTER 15

Impatient for an injection of caffeine, Alyssa blew on the steam rising from her triple-shot vanilla latte. She'd already singed her tongue on her first sip. Her eyelids weighed fifty pounds from yet another sleepless night.

Last night when the guys had gone inside, she'd asked Sophie to meet her at Java Palace this morning. Sophie waved from the doorway and headed to the counter to order. Alyssa's shoulders relaxed: her sister-in-law would be able to help her. She was sure of it.

A few minutes later, Sophie slid into the seat opposite her in the cozy booth tucked into the café's back corner. Privacy was imperative, and this place was consistently full of familiar faces.

"Spill it. I'm dying to know what's going on." Sophie propped her elbows on the scarred wood table. "It's Brandt, isn't it?"

She pressed one hand to her throat. "What? Are you clairvoyant?"

Sophie rolled her eyes. "No, I'm just not blind. Oh my

God, the heat was pumping off you two last night. I'm used to your bickering, but this was different."

"Crap. Do you think Nick noticed?"

Sophie shook her head. "I don't think so, he would have said something. Is that what you're worried about?"

"Yeah. Nick acts like some Regency-era aristocrat intent on finding the best match for his debutante sister. Nobody is ever good enough. At this rate, I'll be single forever. And even though Brandt's his best friend, I think he might kill him if he knew…" She snapped her mouth shut.

"Knew what?" Sophie's sapphire blue eyes narrowed

Alyssa smoothed a strand of hair back and placed her cup into the saucer. "Promise me this is between us. You can't tell Nick."

"I promised you last night when you asked me to meet you. But yes, I promise."

"Well, let me go back a bit. I've had a crush on Brandt for years. I'm talking when I was still in high school." She squeezed her eyes closed. "I think I've compared every guy I've dated to him."

"Hold on one second. My latte is ready." Sophie hurried over to the counter.

Alyssa took a few fortifying breaths. So far, so good. No secrets revealed or confidences betrayed.

Sophie slid back into the booth. "So you've had a crush on Brandt for a dozen years…keep going."

"Okay, I want you to understand it isn't just a crush. I'm in love with him. Crazy about him. I know he's the one for me."

"Like you believe he's your soulmate?" Sophie's dark eyebrows rose practically to her hairline.

She pressed one hand to her hammering heart. "Yes. I know he is. Back at last year's Christmas party, we kissed under the mistletoe, and it was explosive. Our chemistry was off the charts. I knew then my feelings were real. But after the party, he started avoiding me."

"Until your wedding." She huffed out a breath and inhaled a mouthful of latte. Liquid courage—too bad it didn't have a healthy shot of whiskey in it.

Sophie rested her chin in her hand. "What happened at the wedding?"

She cleared her throat. "I propositioned him."

Sophie's cup clattered onto the table. "You what?"

"I propositioned him. I figured he'd never make a move on me because of Nick. So I asked for two weeks of no-strings-attached sex. You know, to get it out of our systems." She shrugged as if she was sharing something completely ordinary.

Sophie doubled over laughing.

"Shhh…it's not funny." Alyssa glanced around the crowded café, but nobody seemed to be paying attention to them.

"I beg to differ. It's hilarious," Sophie said between snorts of laughter. "You know Nick asked him to watch over you—like a big brother, right?"

Alyssa barked out a laugh. "Yeah, Brandt the Manny. I guess Nick should've warned him about me instead."

"Just a little ironic." Sophie shook her head. "Is that why you were slamming tequila shots like a college spring breaker at the reception?"

She shuddered. "Exactly. Ugh, how did we ever drink those? Anyway, after I caught the bouquet, I dragged him away, threw out my proposal, and kissed him. Another mind-blowing kiss, mind you. Then, he shut me down. He was a total jerk."

Sophie gestured for her to continue.

"So basically, the whole time we've been working together these last few weeks was incredibly tense and awkward. The attraction is definitely mutual, and I know he wants me as bad as I want him. But—"

"But Brandt won't make a move on you because he doesn't want to upset Nick. Right?"

A twinge of guilt flared through her, but she couldn't tell Sophie just how many moves they'd had.

"Something like that. Hell, I told him to be a man and just compartmentalize." Alyssa wished she could follow her own advice. "Anyway, so here I am telling you all of this. Can you help? With bringing Nick around, I mean?"

"Are you really sure about this? Is it love, or is it just sex?" Sophie's expression grew serious.

"I know for me, it is love. Our relationship isn't just physical, but we need the chance to find out. Brandt needs more time. We need more time to date like a regular couple. I mean, Nick loves Brandt, so why can't I?" Her heart tightened in her chest.

"Good point. They are like brothers. I guess it's more about Nick letting go of his unrealistic expectations for you to find Mr. Perfect."

"I know." She swallowed a frisson of guilt because part of Nick's over-the-top protectiveness was due to her former eating disorder. Which Sophie didn't know about. Neither did Brandt for that matter. But she'd finished therapy years ago.

"It would ruin their friendship if you guys have a fling, and he dumps you like all the other women. And what about Tearmann House?" Sophie frowned.

"Well, Nick used to be the other Player of Laguna and it all changed when he met you. Why can't Brandt do the same thing with me?" And wasn't that the question of the hour.

"Excellent point. It's just getting Nick to see it that way." Sophie tapped her fingers against her lips.

"And I think Tearmann House is the least of my worries.

We've been getting it done, despite the awkwardness. We can both be professional." Warmth crept into her cheeks at the flashback of the conference table on Day One.

Alyssa gripped her fingers together under the table. If Nick discovered the affair before they were ready to announce they were a couple--because they *would* be a couple--things could devolve quickly.

"True. And let's be honest. At this point, I don't think anybody would be good enough for you in his mind." Sophie threw up her hands. "So, besides me having a talk with him about not being so protective of you, any ideas so far?"

"Maybe you could get pregnant? And I could be an auntie and babysit all the time." She winked.

"Ha, ha. No babies for a while. Like I told you before, I plan on enjoying being a newlywed. Okay, let me try and cook up a plan today."

"Come on, no ideas? You're the creative one here. Can't you fabricate a plot?" She needed a plan. Pronto.

"Off the top of my head, I'm not really sure. Hmm…how about we go on a double date, and you bring a total loser, so in comparison Brandt will seem like a paragon of virtue?"

"Ooooh, what a great idea. Lord knows there are a million of them online. But do we find someone to play the part or just pick a total tool and let the evening run its course?" Alyssa rubbed her hands together.

"Do you know anyone who would do you a favor and play the dirtbag? Or maybe we could have a barbecue and you could bring the guy?"

"Hmm, maybe a get-together works better. And I'll see who I can find online. Damn, I wish Nick and Brandt weren't so stubborn." Understatement of the century.

"Let's ponder this idea today. But first, do tell—did you guys hook up while we were gone? Last night was steamy." Sophie arched her brows.

How much could she reveal? "Maybe you didn't notice before because you didn't know?"

"No, you guys were always snarky or ignored each other. Last night was different. Spill it. I swear I won't tell Nick."

"Pinky swear?" She crossed her legs and toes under the table.

Sophie reached out, and they hooked pinky fingers and laughed. "Done."

"Okay, we kissed again, but he freaked out and rejected me. I think it's why he ran away to San Francisco. He felt guilty and didn't want to face Nick." All of this was the truth, but just a matter of degree…she wouldn't betray Brandt.

"Men." Sophie sighed. "Well, you helped me and Nick, and I'll help you. I think you and Brandt would be awesome together. I think he's got a heart of gold. We'll just nudge those Laguna playboys a little."

"You're the best. I'm off to Tearmann House now. How do I look?" She stood and twirled in a slow circle on her patent leather stilettos, her green silk shirtdress flaring.

Sophie flipped both thumbs up. "Brandt doesn't stand a chance."

ALYSSA ARRIVED AT TEARMANN HOUSE, anticipation dancing along her skin. Bolstered by her newly hatched plan, she strolled into the building, her head held high. Brandt was meant to be hers, and she'd break down his walls, one by one.

She strode down the hall toward the conference room where she'd set up a makeshift workspace for herself. Pulling her laptop and phone out of her briefcase, she prepared to find the worst online date available. Because she didn't have a guy friend she could pitch into the shark tank.

Scott popped his head in the door. "Hi, Alyssa."

"Hey, Scott, how's it going?" Hmm, Scott had been hitting on her subtly and not so subtly since they'd met. Could he be the candidate? No, he was a nice guy, and she certainly didn't need to create issues between him and his boss.

"Everything's great on my end. Brandt will be back tomorrow, so let's have a quick meeting then? Unless you need anything?"

"No, I'm fine today. Thanks." She swallowed the disappointment she wouldn't see Brandt today after all.

Time to go fishing on one of the dating sites. How hard could it be? Orange County was chock-full of superficial men. The litany of atrocious dates she'd endured with men obviously looking for a one-night stand made her cringe. She'd just pick the smarmiest guy she could find and parade him in front of Nick and Brandt.

With a decisive nod, she shot Sophie a text. She immediately replied and suggested a small "we're home from our honeymoon and ready to see other people" barbecue Saturday night. She'd personally ensure that Nick insist Brandt attend.

This endeavor was better suited to her house, so she'd work from home. She now had a few days to find a dirtbag. She packed up her belongings and headed out.

A few hours later, she dropped her forehead onto her desk and groaned. Who were these guys? And how could she get one to go to a family barbecue on a first date? She'd swiped through hundreds, and the dearth of choices depressed her.

First, Tad—who the hell was named Tad—had invited her to a strip club where his sister, yes, his sister, worked. That way, they could get discounted drinks and watch the show. Nothing creepy about a brother watching his sister work a pole. Um, no, thank you very much.

Next, there was Colin, who invited himself over to her

house so she could make him dinner. Delicious food was of utmost importance to Colin, and if she couldn't cook, there wasn't going to be a second date. Well, dear Colin, there wouldn't be a first date.

And by the way, she was a spectacular cook.

There were lewd suggestions, mind-numbingly boring suggestions, and seemingly normal suggestions. Just no real prospect for a barbecue. So much for her brilliant scheme. Damn, damn, damn. What was she going to do? She paced around her living room.

Her phone pinged. She snatched it off the table, and a guy popped up on the screen with a toothy grin, a handsome face, and an innocuous greeting. Maybe?

She replied and they carried on a normal, albeit trivial, conversation. He was complimentary and seemed obsessed with learning more about her height, weight, and bra size.

As they texted, she perused his photos, all twenty of them. Most of them were selfies—swim trunks or boxers and even a red-white-and-blue speedo. With waxed eyebrows and chest. And did he have oil slathered on his sculpted, hairless pectorals? She bit back a laugh. Shallow indeed.

He suggested they go for a run, but she parried with an invitation to a casual barbecue with some of her friends.

She swallowed a tinge of guilt at not revealing the fact her draconian brother was the host of said barbecue. But Shallow Steve was perfect: good-looking, overconfident, and definitely superficial. He agreed in a heartbeat. Please don't let him sport the patriotic speedo, or the plan would never work.

They set a rendezvous at a busy Irish pub in town an hour before the barbecue. She notified Sophie of her success and reinvigorated, she settled in to accomplish some actual work.

Operation Brandt stage one: victory.

CHAPTER 16

randt parked his convertible next to the row of cars in Nick's driveway. Just how big was this "casual barbecue"? And why the hell had he allowed Nick to bully him into showing up?

He'd successfully avoided Alyssa since last week--and if he were going to survive, the last thing he needed was to see her again. Kicking the Alyssa habit was proving tougher than the time he'd stopped drinking coffee for a month.

The piercing headaches. The cloud of fog shrouding his brain. The irritability he couldn't shake, even with punishing runs and lengthy surf sessions. Same. Same. Same.

Hell, with Alyssa, he wasn't only suffering caffeine withdrawal--he'd become a damned insomniac. He tossed and turned all night. When he'd inevitably wake up--hard as stone and drenched in sweat--he reached for her, only to find his bed empty.

He squeezed his eyes shut and dropped his forehead to his beloved Corvette's teak steering wheel. Alyssa was different. He craved not only her sexy body but her joyous laugh and her snarky wit. Her big creative brain and her compassionate heart. Every fiber of his being screamed with need—he missed all of her. He'd avoided Tearmann House simply to create some distance, to flush her from his system.

Yeah, right. He thumped his head on the cool wood.

With the caffeine, his symptoms subsided as the weeks dragged on. With Alyssa, they intensified. Tonight would knock him back to day one. Kind of like a twelve-step program where you had to start over from the beginning again after one slip up.

Like the way at one of the many foster homes over his childhood, the "mother" had never made it past step one. Granted he was used to his parents who'd never even admitted their daily drinking was a problem. And when he ended up on the streets? Addiction and violence were common. He sat up and scrubbed his hands through his hair and blew out a steadying breath.

Keeping Alyssa at arm's distance was the only way he could protect her from himself. Sure, he wasn't a violent guy and had certainly never hurt a woman physically. But he'd never let any woman in as close as he had with Alyssa. And what if he ended up truly being his father and mother's son? His gut clenched––he'd never be able to live with himself if he truly harmed her.

And Nick had ranted about her bringing some dude she'd met online. What the hell? Last week she'd been furious with him, insisting they were meant to be together, and she was already out with another guy? Something unfamiliar twisted in his chest.

Nick had been fired up, insisting they check him out and kick him out if he was a loser. He'd made a half-ass attempt to reassure his best friend that his little sister was an adult and could make her own choices. But yeah, she had chosen him, and he'd pushed her away. The whole situation was a fucking mess.

Enough. No way could he bail on Nick, especially since he'd been keeping secrets from him. He shoved the car door open. No more hiding out. He'd have a beer and burger and head home.

Maybe he'd get lucky, and Alyssa wouldn't be there.

Her laughter reached him first. No, he wasn't getting lucky—in any sense of the word. She had the most melodic laugh, as if sunshine was a sound. His stomach constricted again.

Damn, he had it bad.

Then every muscle in his body stiffened. She appeared in his line of vision, all mile-long tanned legs enhanced by some white shorts the size of a postage stamp and spike-heeled red booties.

When some tall dude in a skin-tight muscle shirt rested his hand on her ass, his vision blurred. What the hell? He charged.

"Brandt…hey, Brandt." Someone caught his arm. "Slow down and get a beer."

Sophie's voice extinguished his progress like a fire hose to the face. Sucking in a deep breath, he harnessed his last shard of self-control.

"Hi, gorgeous. Where's Nick?" He gave Sophie, his second favorite woman in the world, a one-armed hug. Worked to smooth out his breathing.

"He's over by the grill, and I'm sure he wants you to join him cooking over fire like manly men." She laughed and squeezed his arm.

"Who's that loser with Alyssa?" *So much for playing it cool.*

A line appeared between Sophie's brows. "Loser? Be nice. He's good-looking, successful, and seems into her. But I can't remember his name."

"Good-looking? He looks cheesy to me. And why is his hand on her ass?" Okay, maybe from this angle, the dude's hand wasn't on her ass, but her lower back. Still too damn close.

Sophie's lips twitched. "His hand isn't on her ass. And why do you care anyway?"

"Nick wanted me to look out for her. And that guy's gotta go." He lurched forward, and she caught his arm again in a surprisingly strong grip.

Laughter bubbled in her voice. "No you don't. Nice big-brother act, though."

His breath caught. "What?"

"Brandt. You have feelings for her, don't you?"

"What?" He shrugged a shoulder. "No, she's like a little sister." *Yeah, right.*

Sophie rolled her eyes. "Sure, whatever. But you can't go storming over there. You'll embarrass yourself and Alyssa."

"Fine. One move and he's out of here, though." He turned around and headed to get a cold beer. Maybe he should just climb into the fridge. No way he could talk to Nick until he cooled off.

He popped the lid off a microbrew and took a deep pull, willed the beverage to douse the heat steaming through his veins. He downed another mouthful, then stalked to the enormous gas-range grill and joined Nick.

"Did you get a load of the loser with your sister? Give me the word and I'll boot him out of here." Apparently, he'd lost his damn mind.

Nick shrugged and flipped a burger. "Nah, a guy like that's got no chance with her. My sister is definitely picky, and she'll be bored in an hour if she isn't already."

He glared across the clusters of people. "Dude, he looks like a full-on player."

"I don't know why the hell she'd bring him here, but I'm not worried—seriously, not a threat."

"I don't like the look of him." *Get your shit together, Brandt.*

"What are you muttering about?" Nick turned to look at him, and his eyes widened. "Man, you look like shit. Are you sick or something?"

"No, just haven't been sleeping great. And I need another beer. Want one?" Damn it. He should've pretended to have the flu and gotten the hell out of there.

"I'm good."

He'd taken two steps toward the kitchen before Alyssa and the loser blocked his path. Now the guy had his arm around her, and she was snuggled in close to his side.

What. The. Hell?

He jerked to a stop, at a loss for words. He gripped his empty beer bottle. Annoyance flared down his spine.

"Hi, Brandt. When did you make it back in town?" Alyssa kept her fingers wrapped around Steve's paltry forearm, her voice light.

Brandt ground his molars, unable to admit he hadn't been out of town again, just avoiding her.

Her plump pink lips curved upward. "Anyway, I wanted you to meet Steve. I think you guys have a lot in common."

A lot in common—what the hell was that supposed to mean?

Steve extended one well-manicured hand. "Hey, man, nicc to meet you."

Brandt glanced down at the guy's hairless arm––was that oil making it shiny? With a grimace, he shook his cold limp hand.

Then he remembered how close the guy's hand had been to Alyssa's perfect ass. "What are you doing here?" He crossed his arms.

"Huh?" Steve puffed up like a rooster at dawn. "Alyssa's my date. What's your problem?"

"Brandt. You aren't my babysitter. Anymore, that is." She

leaned in closer to the little rooster and stroked his shiny bicep.

Brandt hissed out a breath. Struggled to tamp down his temper. What kind of game was she playing tonight? And when had it gotten so warm outside?

"Come on, Steve. No need to indulge my brother's idiot friend. Let's get some food." She slid her arm through Steve's and with a narrow glance over her shoulder, she sauntered away.

Brandt marched directly to the kitchen and grabbed another beer. He slammed the refrigerator shut for good measure. He rubbed the icy bottle along his forehead, willing the bile in his throat to subside.

Was this part of his penance? He'd been a jerk and not treated her how she deserved. Yeah, he knew it would hurt but was this what jealousy felt like? Because it was new, and he hated it. No way could he have anticipated how awful it would be to see Alyssa cozying up to some sleazeball?

He popped off the lid and took a long sip. He'd make damn sure not to run into her again tonight. If he'd thought he'd be over Alyssa anytime soon, he'd been sorely mistaken.

CHAPTER 17

"What's your deal? Are you always this rude, or is it just with me?" Alyssa addressed Brandt's back. Tried to ignore how hot he looked in his dark jeans and faded T-shirt stretched across his muscular torso.

He pivoted to face her and set his beer on the counter. Thunderclouds darkened his expression, his eyes a stormy midnight blue. "What are you trying to prove?"

She flashed a fake smile and swallowed a giggle. Her plan was working--he was jealous of Steve. "Prove? Nothing. You and I had a good time. It's over. Time to move on, right?"

Although she was baiting the angry bear, she couldn't stop herself. He deserved it after the way he'd acted. The pompous ass.

With a growl, he lunged forward, caught her wrist, and tugged her out of the kitchen and down the hallway. He whipped open the closest door and dragged her into a guest bedroom. He slammed the door and flicked the lock.

"I will not have you dating some loser." He glared at her, his hands gripping her shoulders.

Heat flamed in her cheeks, her temper flaring to match

his. She struggled to escape but he wasn't softening his hold. "You don't want me, but you don't want me to be with someone else? Are you kidding me right now?"

"Don't want you?" His nostrils flared and his pupils flared. "Don't want you?" he hissed. "Oh, screw it." He yanked her closer and captured her lips in a punishing kiss.

For a moment she remained immobile. Wasn't this what she wanted? To make him so jealous he couldn't hide his true feelings? For him to lose control? Why did his roughness send tingles shooting straight down to her center?

His touch gentled, and he slanted his mouth against hers. Tenderness replaced force. He pressed featherlight kisses around her mouth. "Alyssa, please let me in," he murmured.

Her arms wound around his neck, and she threaded her fingers into his thick, wavy hair. Her lips parted and she welcomed his tongue tangling and dancing with hers. *Finally.* His delicious taste enveloped her with hints of salt and sun.

His hands were everywhere at once, rough and desperate, stroking down her back, sliding up her waist, pinching her sensitive nipples––the way he knew drove her wild. A hair shy of pain, but all pleasure. His rock-hard cock dug into her belly, and she rocked closer.

Time stood still, and the sounds of the party faded away as he became her entire world. *This.* This man was all she'd ever wanted. Ever would want.

Her one true love.

He couldn't fight it forever.

His hands slid underneath her whisper-thin T-shirt and tugged down her lacy bra when a loud rattle startled them. When the doorknob jiggled, accompanied by a sharp knock on the door, Brandt lifted his mouth from hers, his breath ragged.

"Alyssa? Are you in there?" Sophie demanded.

Brandt placed his finger against her lips and shook his head. She struggled to regain control of her breathing.

"I saw you two go in there. Let me in right this minute." She sounded like an irate principal corralling a recalcitrant student. As if she meant business.

Brandt's eyes were intense as they bored into her. The bulge in his jeans wasn't subsiding, but she couldn't ignore her sister-in-law. Alyssa disentangled herself from his arms and adjusted her top.

Sophie hammered again.

"I have to let her in. I'm sorry," Alyssa whispered. Damn it all. Could the timing be any worse?

She unlocked the door, cracked it open a hair, and peeked out. Sophie shoved the door wide, elbowed her way inside, and clicked the lock into place.

Hands on her hips, she stared at them both. Alyssa looked down at her feet and dared a glance at Brandt under her lashes. With his eyes downcast and his hands jammed into the front pockets of his jeans, he resembled a little kid waiting to be scolded.

Sophie was as intimidating as the headmaster at her former high school. Who knew? Alyssa bit her lip to prevent herself from giggling. This wasn't funny, was it?

"Okay, you two, spill it," Sophie said, her hands still on her hips.

"There's nothing—"

"What do you mean?" Brandt said simultaneously.

Alyssa struggled to smother the laughter. She'd always laughed when she got in trouble or became nervous. She dug her fingernails into her palms. Under no circumstance could she look over at him again.

"Look, I saw you grab Alyssa and drag her in here, Brandt. Well, after the nice little conversation"—Sophie made air quotes— "you had with her date, who by the way is frantically scurrying around the backyard looking for her as we speak."

"I—" Crap. What if Sophie spilled their secret to Nick? Brandt obviously wasn't ready for that. If he ever would be.

Sophie held up her hand. "I'm not finished. I saw you and who knows who else did too. I know Nick didn't, or he'd be ripping the door down right now. So if you want me to help you two get out of this jam, spill it."

Damn, she was scary when she was serious. No wonder her brother was head over heels. But what to say?

Brandt had changed the game tonight when he'd hauled her off like a Neanderthal into the locked bedroom. She recalled his possessive growl and rough hands on her, and heat bloomed low in her belly.

If only her sister-in-law hadn't interrupted them, they'd be making excellent use of the guest bed by now... She braved a look at Brandt, and his ocean-blue gaze was distant. He gave a tiny shake of his head.

Her shoulders sagged, and her stomach dropped. Why had he lost all self-control if he didn't care? Why couldn't he be brave enough to fight for her? To stand up to Nick and tell him he cared about her? At least tell Sophie?

"Sophie, look, Nick asked me to watch out for her." He retreated and held up both hands. "I just don't like the look of the guy, and I wanted to make sure Alyssa could see reason. That's all. No need to mention it to Nick. You know how he is."

He focused all his attention on Sophie. Abandoning her again. Ignoring her completely. Leaving her alone.

Sophie's gaze bounced between them. "Seriously? That's your best story? I would've thought better of you, Brandt. Alyssa?"

Her throat tightened. "He's right. Nothing is going on. Nothing at all." She'd sworn it would be their secret but couldn't have conceived how high a price she'd pay for the promise.

ALYSSA GULPED down more wine and waited for Nick to hand her a plate of food. Steve buzzed inanely in her ear, and she resisted the urge to swat him away like a pesky mosquito. What a dumb idea to bring him. Yeah, she had acted like a teenager and had the results to show for it. Although Brandt had definitely reacted, her plot seemed to have backfired.

No question he'd been jealous. A frisson of excitement sparked down her spine recalling his forceful embrace. Responding to Brandt's alpha-male display, she'd almost combusted in the bedroom. Why couldn't he admit he wanted to be with her? Even just to Sophie?

"Earth to Alyssa—hey." Nick waved the spatula in front of her face. "Here's your veggie burger. What is up with you tonight?"

"Nothing, nothing. Just a little distracted, that's all. Where's your wife? Run away from you now the honeymoon's over?" Time to deflect his attention.

Her stomach coiled into ropes. Nick was hypersensitive to her former eating disorder. She couldn't exactly say, "Never fear. It's not another bout of anorexia. I'm just devastated because Brandt won't admit we've been having hot monkey sex and he's my soulmate. My deepest fear of becoming a spinster aunt to you and Sophie's children appears imminent on the horizon. It kind of kills the appetite."

"Very funny, brat. She's walking over as we speak." His stern expression transformed into a goofy grin at his wife's approach.

If only Brandt looked at her the same way. In public anyway. "Aww, I love seeing you two so in love."

Alyssa accepted the plate. When she focused on how happy she was for them, she could relegate her obsession with her disastrous love life to the back corner of her heart. No need to resurrect her boarding school acting skills tonight.

"Burger or chicken?" Nick shifted his narrowed gaze to her date.

Her date stood sipping his cocktail, managing to flex his chiseled arms each time he lifted the glass to his lips. Yeah, her plot rated a giant fail. He retreated a step at Nick's fierce expression.

"A burger would be great. No bun. Thanks, man." Steve offered a tentative smile but maintained his distance.

Alyssa glanced over at him and forced a smile. Despite confirming her initial impression he was boring and narcissistic, he seemed harmless.

"Hurry up big brother. My burger's going to be cold." Sophie had almost reached them––no need for another confrontation tonight.

Nick handed over the plate, and they made their escape to a picnic table just before Sophie reached the grill.

"So where'd you disappear to?" Steve asked.

Never mind that he wasn't looking in her direction because he was focused on stripping the cheese from his burger with the precision of a neurosurgeon.

"Oh, just caught up with an old friend. Sorry. Didn't mean to be rude." It wasn't a lie, was it? Catching up was accurate and Brandt *had* at one time been a friend.

Once Steve's burger was sufficiently denuded of any carbohydrates or fat, he took a bite. "No worries. Your stems look amazing in those shorts. What do you think of going for a run tomorrow to keep them toned?"

Unfortunately, she'd just taken a sip of wine— couldn't stomach the veggie burger quite yet—and choked. Stems? Keep her legs toned? Wow, big surprise the guy was single.

She cleared her throat and resolved to be kind because, after all, she had used him tonight. "I've got plans tomorrow, but thanks for the offer. And actually, I do need to make it an early night tonight. Do you mind leaving soon?"

He frowned. "Can I finish my burger?"

"Of course, no need to rush. It's just been a long week, that's all." Time to retreat to her apartment and indulge in a steaming bubble bath and more wine. Alone.

He shrugged; eyes still glued to his dinner.

While he nibbled at a snail's pace, she scanned the small crowd in the backyard. No sign of Brandt. Had he gone home? Her shoulders drooped as the impact of the evening sank in.

No more ridiculous schemes to try to make Brandt see they belonged together. Life didn't work that way— you couldn't force anyone to do anything. You certainly couldn't force love. Although, dammit, he'd displayed he cared a million ways over the last few weeks.

And he couldn't conceal his jealousy tonight. What else was he hiding? He'd told her about his tragic childhood, but he was a successful adult now. What was holding him back besides Nick? If he really wanted her and they presented a united front, Nick would have to come around eventually. She was his only sister. Right?

Steve interrupted her musings. "Let's head out. Are you sure you don't want to grab another drink?"

"No drink, but yes, let's go." What part of I'm tired and I have to go home didn't he get?

She glanced toward the grill, and Brandt stood next to her brother, laughing with him and Sophie as if he didn't have a care in the world. Never in a million years would anyone think this carefree surfer dude had exploded with fury and dragged her into a room like a pirate absconding with forbidden bounty.

Maybe he'd win this year's Oscar for best actor.

Unable to muster the energy for another encounter with Brandt, she waved at the three of them. She turned and grabbed Steve's arm and headed to the car.

Best to leave this battleground in the rearview. Operation Brandt had to be chalked up in the loss column, at least for tonight.

CHAPTER 18

*B*randt had escaped out of the bedroom as soon as Principal Sophie unlocked the door. He half-jogged down the hall to the bathroom and locked himself inside. He pulled the sink stopper, turned the water on cold, and once the basin was full, dunked his head in. The freezing temperature slammed into him, but he held his breath until his lungs practically exploded.

He ripped his head out of the icy water and grabbed the closest towel to dry his drenched head. Once he'd scrubbed most of the water out of his hair, he made the mistake of glancing down. He recoiled in horror at the fluffy monogrammed terry cloth. Nick now had monogrammed guest towels?

He shook his head again, like Bailey after a bath, and stared at himself in the mirror. Sucked in a breath. He did look like shit.

One glance at Alyssa with another guy and he'd lost it. Gotten forceful. Hell, that first kiss hadn't been in attraction. It'd been in anger. Rough. Violent. How could she even look at him, much less respond to him? He gripped the marble sink and squeezed his eyes shut.

When he opened them, his scumbag of a father stared back at him in the reflection. Fate must've chuckled when it molded him into the spitting image of his vicious, criminal dad. Most of the time, he didn't notice it. Refused to acknowledge the resemblance. But now with his eyes bloodshot and his face drawn, he couldn't deny it. How deep did the similarities go?

What had he been thinking? He'd been inexcusably rough with her, and it served up an intense reminder he came from shit. He wasn't good enough for her. Would never be good enough for her. No matter how she clung to this romanticized version of him.

She didn't deserve some loser who could get violent so easily. He'd never be able to live with himself if he actually did hurt her. He needed to pull it together and make a plan to distance himself from her. This time for good.

Step one: go hang out with Nick and act as if everything was normal. Nick couldn't suspect what had happened. He'd convince him life was rolling on as usual, casual and carefree.

If only he could convince himself.

With one last shake of his head, he returned to the party.

When Alyssa departed with her date, Brandt managed not to watch her leave. Not counting his peripheral vision.

He gave himself a mental pat on the back. He could do this. He ignored Sophie's frequent glances at him. He refused to engage—the less she knew, the less opportunity for Nick to discover anything. If he lost Nick, he'd no longer have a family.

"Not sure why she'd give that guy the time of day, much

less bring him over here, but at least he seemed harmless." Nick shrugged.

"Another one bites the dust," Sophie mused.

Brandt sipped his beer. Remained silent. Safer that way.

Nick's gaze swung his way. "So you're sure everything was okay with her while we were gone, right?"

Sophie raised an eyebrow at him but said nothing.

"Dude, I told you. She's fine. She's doing a great job at the center." Brandt fought the panic bubbling in his gut.

"Okay, okay. Sorry. I just don't want her to get hurt."

Sophie rubbed his shoulder. "Nick, you can't control her life. Let her live it. Let her make her own mistakes. If you're too overbearing, she'll start keeping secrets from you, and is that what you want?"

"Secrets? What secrets? Do you know something?" His voice grew louder, and he swiveled to look down at his wife.

She laughed and hugged him. "No, silly, just reminding you she's an adult and independent and doesn't need to be worried about meeting whatever crazy high expectations you have of her. Just let her be."

Nick frowned. "I'm not that bad, am I?"

Brandt and Sophie both laughed. Hopefully, neither caught the bitterness tingeing his tone. "Enough family time, guys. I'm outta here." Brandt backed away with a wave, eager to escape.

"Give me a hug before you go. After all, aren't you my new brother?" Sophie smiled slyly at him.

He hugged her, and she whispered in his ear, "Go get her, tiger."

He stiffened and stepped back from her, his gaze swinging to Nick. Luckily, he hadn't appeared to hear his wife's suggestion.

Shit. He could never go get her.

Instead, he got in the car and headed home. Alone.

CHAPTER 19

*A*lyssa blinked repeatedly at the computer screen to bring the room design she'd been working on into focus. Not happening. Defeated, she pulled up her calendar for the hundredth time since eight a.m. She ticked the days off on her fingers and jotted the numbers onto her yellow scratch pad.

Thirty-two. No matter how she calculated, the numbers stubbornly refused to add up to anything other than thirty-two. Thirty-two days since her last period.

Crap, crap, *crap*.

Huffing out her breath, she thunked her head onto the desk. Her belly cramped, and her heart ached. What was she going to do?

She sat back in the chair and stared at the piece of paper. Still thirty-two. Still too many.

Although her period had become irregular when her weight plummeted in high school and college, she'd learned to manage her triggers. After years in therapy and support groups, she'd learned to funnel her anxiety into positive arenas like yoga and meditation. Up until this month, her period ran like clockwork.

Until Brandt, her period had run like clockwork.

She squeezed her eyes shut and fought against hyperventilating. She hadn't panted like this since the last time she'd made the mistake of sashaying into an advanced spin class. She counted to five on her inhale and exhaled for five. She repeated the breath pattern, willing her heartbeat to slow down.

She couldn't be pregnant. Of course, she wasn't pregnant. She was hyper-tuned to her body, and she'd know. Wouldn't she? She rubbed her belly and detected no telltale bump.

They'd been diligent and used protection every single time. Hadn't they? No evidence of a broken soldier.

This was absolutely not happening.

Brandt couldn't even stand up to her brother to date her, so how would he react to the prospect of being her baby daddy? He'd never had a committed relationship, so the odds were definitely not in her favor he'd be excited about impending parenthood.

But he was an honorable guy. Right?

She contemplated her brother's face if and when they'd have to tell him they'd gotten pregnant. After he'd asked Brandt to be her babysitter. To protect her. Bile rose in her throat, and she choked the bitter taste down. Nick would murder him. Slowly and painfully. And Brandt would probably let him, the martyr. Crap.

A staccato beat hammered in her temples. No way could she sit here another minute. She'd go to the drugstore and pick up a pregnancy test. Or five. Decision made. She rose from the chair and sank back into the seat a moment later. No way could she go to the local store where she knew everyone, and everyone knew her.

Maybe wait a few more days? She had been under an

undue amount of stress since Nick and Sophie returned from their honeymoon. Who was she kidding? She'd been unable to eat or sleep or relax since Operation Brandt Barbecue blew up in her face.

Warmth filled her cheeks at the memory of him dragging her into the nearest bedroom and kissing her senseless. The depth of his passion blew her away. Then, nothing. This week, he'd pulled a Houdini. Not a peep nor even a perfunctory appearance at Tearmann House. Chicken. Coward or not, she loved him.

And she loved the idea of a little boy or girl with his gorgeous blue eyes and dark hair. A bundle of unconditional love. How she wanted to start a family with him, to spend her life with him.

No more waffling. Pushing away from the table, she sprung to her feet and grabbed her briefcase. Not another second, she had to know now. If she headed down to Dana Point or even up to Newport Beach, she'd be anonymous. Alone. Safe to buy up all the pregnancy tests until she was convinced either way.

She charged for the door, intent to go before she changed her mind. And smacked into a rock-hard chest. Gasping, she retreated.

"Alyssa?" Brandt's voice was quiet. He grasped her shoulders.

She yanked out of his grip and stepped back. Her already-tense belly flip-flopped.

"Are you okay?" he asked when she failed to utter a syllable.

"Just peachy. Like you care." Sarcasm scored her tone, but too bad. Did he think she'd just bounce right back after the barbecue?

His poker face slid into place, and his eyes cooled. "Of course I care."

"You have a funny way of showing it." She narrowed her eyes. The pounding in her temples became excruciating. No way was she having this discussion before she'd taken the test.

"We've been through this. Nothing has changed. I want you to be happy, and that can't happen if I'm anything more than your honorary big brother." His eyes chilled into two ice chips.

"Oh please." She snorted. "What a joke—big brother, especially now…" We might be pregnant. She snapped her mouth shut.

His gaze flicked away, but despite the gentling of his tone, his expression failed to soften. "I'm sorry about the other night. I know I was an ass."

"Yeah, you were. Look, I need to leave now." Needed to escape.

"Now? It's only two o'clock." He cocked a brow.

"You haven't been here all week, and you're worried about when I come and go?" She couldn't tell him. Not like this. Not when they were acting like strangers.

She stormed toward the door, intent only on putting distance between them before she lost her composure completely.

"Hold on, Alyssa. We need to find a new normal. We need to finish Tearmann House, and I can't keep walking on eggshells around you, damn it." He sounded impatient. Irritated. As if she were some petty problem to be handled.

She swallowed the scream bubbling up into her throat. "Eggshells? Eggshells…"

"Calm down." His tone grated. As if he were handling a toddler or an out-of-control puppy.

"Don't you be condescending to me. Damn you, I won't calm down." How dare he treat her like a hysterical female? Even though she was on the brink of losing her shit.

Fine. It looked as if they were doing this now. She marched the last few steps to the door, slammed it, and locked it.

Eggshells, my ass.

She paused, unable to turn toward him quite yet. She hugged her arms around her waist. If a single nerve in her body weren't on full alert, she'd be shocked.

How was she going to do this when he'd made it so clear they were done? "I need to tell you something…"

"Alyssa, what is it?" Concern colored his voice.

She headed toward the table and perched on the edge of a chair. "Sit down and I'll tell you. It's probably nothing."

Brandt leaned his weight against the conference table, crossing one ankle over the other and crossing his arms. Yeah, a body language expert would have a field day with his posture. His expression revealed nothing. He gestured with one hand for her to continue.

"I'm late." She gazed down at her hands.

"Late?" He frowned. "Late for what?"

"Four days late." She blinked her eyes furiously. No way would she cry in front of him again.

"I wasn't serious about Tearmann. We have plenty of time—"

"Damn it, Brandt. My period is late. I might be pregnant." The words flooded out of her in a rush.

He stared at her like a deer in headlights. Then he smacked his hand on the conference table, levered away from it, and stalked across the room.

He raked his hands through his hair. "That's impossible. We used protection. You can't be pregnant."

She stared at his rigid back. Dug her nails into her palms, desperate to cling to her last shard of self-control. "I'm usually like clockwork…"

He pivoted back to face her. "Four days? How could you know in four days? What are you trying to pull?"

"I'm never late." The pounding in her forehead compressed into an excruciating vise. "And what do you mean what am I trying to pull?"

"You're trying to manipulate me into a relationship? Into telling Nick?" He glared, his eyes no longer glacial, but burning blue flames.

Her breath caught in her throat. "Manipulate you?"

"You heard me. I refuse to tell Nick about us and now this? I won't be manipulated. This doesn't change anything." His jaw clenched.

"This?" She shook her head and looked around. Was she in the midst of a nightmare? Nope, still in the Tearmann House conference room.

"If you're pregnant. If this is some misguided attempt to convince me we should be in a relationship. This. Doesn't. Change. Anything." He bit the words out, his face suddenly unfamiliar.

Impending tears evaporated, and fury surged through her veins. He was not accusing her of playing the pregnancy card to force him to go public with her, was he?

"You arrogant ass. How dare you. Misguided attempt? Like I would pretend to be pregnant?" She bit back a scream. "Why don't you just accuse me of poking holes in the condoms?"

A muscle in his jaw twitched. "Well, you started all of this, pushed me, kept secrets. How am I supposed to trust you?"

Each word fell like a blow. The well-placed barb struck its mark and her heart cracked. She pressed her hands against her belly, struggling for composure. Did he really think so little of her?

"Look, I'm sorry. You can't be pregnant. And if somehow

the protection failed, we'll handle it." His voice had gentled, but it drifted toward her from miles away.

"Handle it?" Her voice rose precariously high. "What exactly does handle it mean?"

His nostrils flared. "I told you I'd never have children. Not with you, not with anyone. I won't be forced into marriage, into being a father, not even for you. I'll leave Laguna if I have to."

"You know what family means to me, Brandt—" The arrow in her heart twisted deeper. She crossed the space between them and slapped his face. He caught her wrist.

His face was carved from marble, hard, smooth, and devoid of any warmth. "I do, but not with me. Never with me. You know this."

"Am I so repulsive you refuse to share this with me? How can you be so cold?"

"It's not you. It's me. I can't be a father. I won't have children. I—" His mouth snapped shut and he stepped away from her.

Tears threatened again as the pain superseded her burst of anger. Who was he? "Oh, the 'it's not you, it's me' again? Seriously?"

He turned toward the door. "I'm serious."

"Can't or won't be a father?" Was it possible to feel your heart shatter in your chest?

Brandt shrugged a shoulder but refused to meet her gaze. "Does it matter? Can't, won't."

"Yeah, you're making yourself clear." And another piercing pain in her chest.

He finally looked at her, his eyes chips of frozen glass. "Look, this is probably just a scare. Stress. The odds are low. Have you even taken a test?"

"That's where I was going when you came in. Well, don't

worry about it. I'm not your concern. If I am pregnant, I'll raise the child on my own. No need for you to be involved."

He turned fully and extended one hand. "No, I—"

"I'll do what I please, and you can go straight to hell."

Snatching up her briefcase, she stalked to the door, praying she could make it to her car without losing her composure completely. She fumbled with the lock, cursing her clumsy fingers. Finally, she managed to fling the door open.

"Regardless of what the test says, I don't ever want to see you again. I quit." She slammed the door and fled to her car. Tears streamed down her face as she managed to dive into the driver's seat and screech out of the parking lot. Away from him. Forever.

CHAPTER 20

*A*lyssa peeled out onto the road, the pressure behind her eyes threatening to blind her vision. Her right leg trembled, and her foot couldn't seem to stay steady on the gas pedal. A parking space miraculously materialized, and she pulled in, knowing it wasn't safe for her to drive yet. She cut the engine and rested her throbbing forehead on the steering wheel.

Tears burned tracks down her cheeks as Brandt's words ran on repeat like a warped record. Had he really said he'd leave town before being a father to their child? That he'd never be a father? Accused her of trying to manipulate him?

Had she been projecting her own feelings on him? Had it really only been sex? Had she ever known him at all? A quote she'd heard once floated across her mind, something about when someone shows you their true colors, believe them.

Were these Brandt's true colors? She could never imagine being with him now. Not after his reaction. Not after his harsh words. Not after his coldness.

Sitting back, she wiped an errant tear from her cheek and took a cleansing breath. No more waiting and wondering.

Time to head to Dana Point and buy a few pregnancy tests. Whatever the result, she'd deal with it. She turned on the engine.

Before she could shift into drive, her phone rang. Her gut tightened. Brandt? She glanced down, and Sophie's name popped up on the display. She hesitated--no need to complicate the situation further. It was already a disaster.

The phone rang two more times.

Damn it. Maybe Sophie could help. "Hey, Sophie." Alyssa's voice cracked.

"What's wrong? Are you crying?"

So much for composure. "Oh God, everything's a total mess. My life's over. I just quit…"

"Quit? Tearmann House? What? Where are you?"

"I'm parked about a block south of it on S Coast Highway. I was just heading down to Dana Point." She croaked out two full sentences.

"Dana Point? What's going on?" Sophie started talking before she could reply. "No, don't tell me over the phone. Stay right where you are. I'm coming to pick you up. Sit tight. I'm about two minutes away."

"Okay. I'll be here." Alyssa stared out the windshield.

A buzzing sound jolted her out of her trance. Her phone. Oh yeah, Sophie was coming to the rescue.

"I'm right behind you. Leave your car. We'll take mine." Sophie's tone left no room for disagreement.

Grabbing her briefcase, she locked up her car and climbed into Sophie's little compact.

"You look terrible. I'm taking you to my house." Sophie started out into traffic.

"No, no, I can't risk seeing my brother. I need to get out of town. I need to go to the drugstore." Crap, she shouldn't pull her brother's wife into this nightmare. But this seemed too big. Too much to handle alone.

Sophie turned; her eyes wide. "Which is it? A drugstore or out of town?"

"Both. I need to pick up a pregnancy test."

Sophie slammed on the brakes. "What?" She whipped her head toward Alyssa and frowned. "Brandt?"

She bit her lip. "You can't tell Nick."

Sophie's brow creased. "Oh no, is this why you quit?"

"I'll tell you everything, but could you please just drive. I can't risk anybody we know seeing me buying pregnancy tests." Her fingers curled into her palms.

Sophie flicked a hand. "Don't worry about it. I'll buy them. Nobody would question the newlywed."

Alyssa burst into a fresh round of tears. She'd never be a newlywed with Brandt. Probably never get married. She dropped her head into her hands, overwhelmed.

"Oh God, Alyssa, I'm sorry. We'll go to Dana Point. Don't worry. We'll figure everything out." Sophie stomped on the accelerator, speeding south.

Alyssa appreciated her haste. They rode in silence until Sophie pulled into a little strip mall and parked in front of a drugstore.

Sophie rubbed her shoulder. "Let's get the tests first and talk later, okay?"

Alyssa nodded, still unable to trust her ability to speak without bursting into a fresh spate of sobbing. They found the aisle displaying a bewildering variety of pregnancy tests. Unable to decipher which one would be appropriate, Alyssa shrugged at Sophie's baffled expression.

"Oh hell, I'll get one of every brand. Can't hurt, right?" Sophie grabbed the boxes from the shelf, stacking them up to her chin.

"Should we buy something else to camouflage? Maybe some magazines, chips, lip gloss?" Alyssa vacillated between crying and laughing. Was she hysterical, after all?

Sophie headed toward the register. "Um, no. We already look conspicuous. No need to make it worse. Let's go."

Now what?

"Do you want to go to your condo?" Sophie said, reading her mind when they walked outside.

"I don't think I can wait so long…" She looked around the parking lot.

"Well, I refuse to allow you to pee on a stick behind a dumpster, so what about that little coffee house? I've actually been there before, and they have an individual restroom." Sophie gestured to the other end of the shopping center.

They entered the quaint little café, which was blessedly empty except for an older gentleman tucked into a corner booth, reading a book.

Sophie handed Alyssa the brown paper bag. "You go, and I'll order us some tea. Do you want a muffin or anything?"

"I couldn't eat right now if you paid me. I'll be out in a few minutes." She trudged into the restroom, dread twisting her belly.

Once she locked the door, she sought an appropriate spot for her science experiment. A small wooden table adorned with a vase of fake daisies sat against the far wall. Perfect. She moved the plastic flowers onto the floor and plopped down the bag. She fished out all six tests and fumbled with the annoying packaging on the first one.

Didn't they want people to open the damn things? Growling in frustration, she ripped the plastic apart with her teeth and managed to pry it open. One down, five to go.

A giggle bubbled up her throat as she realized she'd have to open all of them and hit all the sticks in one fell swoop. Or stream. What a ridiculous situation. Sneaking out of town to pee on sticks in a coffeehouse. Could be a country music song.

Not exactly how she'd envisioned getting pregnant for the first time.

Two broken fingernails and a paper cut on her lip later, she managed to hit the bull's eye on each test. She arranged the finished products on a few paper towels, with the corresponding directions beneath each one.

"Here goes nothing," she murmured, setting the timer on her phone. Each test required a minimum of two to three minutes to reveal how dramatic a turn her life would take.

Why was it when you wanted time to go quickly, it dragged slower than an appointment at the DMV? The Jeopardy theme bounced in her head. Doo-doo-doo-doo, doo-doo-doo…

Tapping her feet, snapping her fingers—nothing worked to accelerate the time. She scowled at her phone's timer, willing it to speed up. After an eternity, the alarm beeped.

She squeezed her eyes shut and inhaled a deep cleansing breath. Whatever the result, she'd handle it. Blinking her eyes open, she gazed down at the tests staring back at her like a city block of row houses with only one window each.

"Here goes nothing." She blew out an enormous sigh.

Test number one greeted her with a single blue line in its window. She grabbed the pamphlet she'd lined up directly below. The photo reflected one line equaled not pregnant.

Her shoulders softened. One by one, she compared the pamphlet photo to the accompanying test result. Not a positive cross or a double line in sight.

Negative. Negative. Negative. Negative. Negative. Negative.

Every single one was negative. Which meant she wasn't pregnant.

Why were her feet frozen to the floor? Shouldn't she be jumping for joy?

A knock on the door jolted her.

"Sorry, sorry. I'll be out in a second," she called over her shoulder, unable to pry her eyes away from the table of no-baby-for-you sticks.

"Alyssa, it's me. You've been in there a really long time. Are you okay?"

Alyssa pivoted from the table and cracked open the door. She grabbed Sophie, dragged her into the bathroom, and slammed the door.

"Well?" Sophie pointed at the table.

Sophie walked over and read the results. "This is good news, right?" She turned and raised her brows.

"Of course. Of course, it is. Especially after the way Brandt reacted. Oh God, I never want to see him again." She closed her eyes again.

Sophie rushed over and hugged her tight. Alyssa absorbed her friend's warmth and strength because no matter how deep she dug, numbness greeted her.

"Forget the tea. Let's get rid of these tests and get out of here. How about we head to Vines and have a glass or four of wine and you can tell me everything that happened? Okay?" Sophie smiled encouragingly at her.

Alyssa shivered. "No, nowhere public. I don't want to run into Christian or Brandt or anyone we know, for that matter."

"You're right." Sophie nodded. "Let's pick up some wine and go to your place. I'll let Nick know we're having some girl time."

"Deal. Thanks so much for being such a good friend." They returned to the car, and Alyssa sank back into the seat, processing the test results and attempting to absorb the pain.

Brandt had told her over and over again he couldn't be with her. She'd been stupid enough not to believe him. Now she did.

They headed north toward Laguna. They drove in silence until Sophie's phone buzzed.

"Oh, it's Kelly. Do you mind if I get it?" Alyssa waved her hand in acquiescence. Sophie popped in her earpiece and answered. The car was quiet while she listened to her friend on the other end of the phone.

"Oh no. I'm so sorry… Now? You're on the road now? Hold on a second." Sophie glanced toward Alyssa.

"Kelly just broke up with her boyfriend and was driving up here to get away for the night. Do you mind if she comes over to your condo too? If not, I can tell her it's not a good time."

Alyssa sighed. Hell, misery loves company, right? And she'd met Sophie's best friend several times and adored her. "Sure, tell her to come over. She needs to pick up chocolate to go with our wine, though. A lot of chocolate."

Sophie nodded, relayed the sugar decree, and clicked off.

"She'll be there in half an hour. Apparently, she bailed from work today too and started driving. Out of character. What's going on in the stars today?"

"Official Men Are Asshats Day?" Alyssa snorted out something that was half sob, half laugh.

"Perfect title. Women around the world, unite. Right? Okay, we need lots of wine and chocolate. We'll make it a slumber party, and I'll tell Nick that Kelly's upset and driving up and it's easier for us to hang at your place."

"I'm sorry to put you in this position with Nick. I'm too selfish to not take you up on it, though." Being alone right now wasn't an option.

Sophie smiled. "Don't worry about it. It isn't lying. I would've made him go out tonight, anyway, if we weren't together and Kelly needed me. Girlfriends are important. He'll be fine."

Alyssa nodded, gratitude filling her heart.

"Do you want me to call any of your other girlfriends to come over?" Sophie asked.

"No, the fewer people who know about this, the better." She shook her head.

She had girlfriends, but more the go-out-with, go-to-yoga-with, or generally hang-out-with type. Nobody who needed to be involved in this Brandt situation. After returning to Laguna from school in Savannah, she'd focused on building her interior design career and enjoyed spending her free time cooking, working out, or going to yoga.

She didn't stay in touch with anyone from her awful boarding school days, and most of her friends from Savannah had remained in the South. She and Nick had always been a tight unit, and neither of them had the easiest time letting people close. Sophie was an exception. She'd clicked with both Morgans, and Alyssa loved her like a sister.

Sophie and her best friend, Kelly lived in different cities now, so she had more time to spend with Alyssa. Thank goodness.

She swallowed the huge lump in her throat. Damn it. She wasn't going to cry again. Where the hell did all the liquid even come from?

Sophie parked in front of the bottle shop and turned to her. "I'll go in and pick up some wine, so you don't have to risk running into anyone, okay?"

"That would be amazing. Yes, please. And chocolate, please." Alyssa forced a smile, touched by her friend's sensitivity.

Alone again, she considered calling Brandt with the test results. Her tummy constricted when she recalled the utter finality of his cruel words. She didn't want to hear his voice. No, he could stew tonight, just as she had for a few days. Why hurry? What did it matter?

Screw him. Maybe she wouldn't bother. Not as if he cared anyway. Had he ever? Where was a sense of relief?

A jackhammer couldn't penetrate the icy shell blocking her heart. She would never be with Brandt again. Time to wake up and move on. No amount of will, or love, or of anything would create a world where they would live happily ever after.

Her vision of Brandt was simply a sham. Although both Brandt and her brother were players, Nick had the courage and heart to love. To move forward and take a chance.

Brandt apparently had no heart. And he definitely chose fear over love.

She dropped her head into her hands and started sobbing again. Even when Sophie returned with a bag of clinking bottles, she couldn't stem the flow. Her friend stroked her hair for a few moments before starting the car and driving them to her condo.

Thank god for great friends who allowed her to wallow in silence.

CHAPTER 21

When Sophie pulled up to the condo, Alyssa scrubbed her hands across her face. Home sweet home. Time to move on to the wine and words portion of the day.

"Kelly's already here. She must have flown up the highway. Come on, let's get you both inside." Sophie patted her leg.

Kelly stepped out of a sensible silver sedan, wearing a conservative navy skirt suit. Usually, Sophie's best friend had a sharp confident air but today, her shoulders slumped, and her eyes were puffy and bloodshot.

"Hey guys." Even her usually melodic voice was colored with sadness.

Sophie hurried over and wrapped her arms around Kelly. "You did come right from the office. It's going to be okay, whatever it is. I've got you."

Alyssa swallowed a tinge of guilt. Poor Sophie—her two closest friends were a mess. So much for allowing her sister-in-law to enjoy the honeymoon period she deserved.

Sophie stepped back and waved the bag filled with wine

bottles. "Okay, ladies, let's get inside. I'll pour us some wine, open the chocolate, and we'll work through this. It's going to get better, I promise."

At least someone felt confident.

Entering her condo, Alyssa flipped on the lights, tossed her purse onto the small foyer table, and kicked off her shoes. "Must change into sweats. Kelly, do you need some comfy clothes?"

Kelly released her long tawny hair from its tight chignon. "I need to get this damn suit off. I had to wear it to court this morning, and I feel like I'm in a straight jacket."

"Never fear, I've got you covered. Come with me." She marched toward her bedroom.

Alyssa dug into her bottom dresser drawer, where her beloved, ancient sweats resided. She picked her favorites and handed Kelly an equally ratty ensemble. Once they both changed, they returned to the living room. Sophie had already poured generous glasses of wine and placed the large box of dark sea-salt caramel chocolate on the coffee table.

Alyssa settled onto the cozy couch, and instantly, her cheeks flushed at the memory of making love to Brandt on this exact spot. Crap, she'd probably have to sell it and get a new one.

For that matter, the carpet and bed had to go as well. Would she have to replace the bathtub, shower, and granite kitchen counter too? Maybe she just needed a lobotomy to forget it all. She peered into her glass of chardonnay, willing it to transform into a crystal ball and provide insight into her murky future.

"Alyssa, are you warm? You look red. Do you want me to turn on the air?" Sophie asked.

Alyssa shook her head. "Nah, I'm fine. Thanks, though." Nowhere near fine.

Sophie rubbed her hands together and glanced between

her and Kelly. "Okay, the doctor is in. Which one of you wants to go first? Tell Dr. Sophie all your problems, and we'll fix them."

Kelly's lips twitched. "You missed your calling as a shrink. Although we better not see this storyline showing up in your next novel. I'm still trying to gather my thoughts and process. Definitely not ready to talk about how my life imploded just yet."

"Alyssa, you go." She waved an arm, the enormous old Cornell hoodie Nick had given Alyssa years ago when he'd still been a student, hanging off her petite frame.

Alyssa took a fortifying breath. "Okay. Well, Sophie knows some of it, but I'll give you the short version.

"So I've always been in love with Brandt. He never noticed until this past Christmas. We kissed under the mistletoe, and our chemistry ruined me. After that, he avoided me or if we saw each other, he was kind of a snarky jerk. But I couldn't forget." She sipped her wine.

Sophie nodded and patted her thigh reassuringly.

Kelly's golden eyes were wide as she reached for a chocolate and gestured with the candy for her to continue.

"So remember I caught the wedding bouquet, thanks to Sophie." She turned and gave her friend a light poke in the chest.

Sophie held up both hands. "Hey, I had no idea about your feelings for Brandt. I just know you're ready to find your person."

Alyssa squeezed her eyes shut for a moment. "I know, I know. Anyway, I figured what the hell. I grabbed Brandt, dragged him off toward the woods, and propositioned him. A two-week fling while Nick and Sophie were gone. We kissed, but then he basically told me it would never happen."

Sophie interjected, "Kelly, you know Nick and Brandt are best friends, but Brandt doesn't have a family so they're more like brothers. Because of the past, Nick's crazy protective of Alyssa, so Brandt didn't want to risk their friendship."

A crease appeared between Kelly's brows, concern apparent on her face. "Got it."

"Anyway, when we started working together at Tearmann House, the situation became a ticking time bomb. Let's just say it detonated, and I had the two most amazing weeks of my life with him. And then…" She gazed down into her wine again. Nope, still not a crystal ball. Not even one of those Magic 8 Balls, for that matter.

"The whole time we were in France?" Sophie asked.

Alyssa's throat tightened. "Yes. I'm so sorry I couldn't confide in you, but he was so worried about betraying Nick, I just couldn't…"

Sophie waved her apology away. "I get it. Then what happened?"

"Well, everything was incredible until the last night. We were having dinner and I just assumed…" Her belly clenched and she took another steadying breath. "I suggested we pick you guys up at the airport together, and he freaked out. Just bolted."

Alyssa smoothed her hair away from her face. The spear of pain in her chest hadn't disappeared. Not at all. "Anyway…"

"So, a few days later we invited them over for dinner, and the tension between the two of them was off the charts. I'm talking steamy." Sophie fanned herself before continuing.

"She confided her feelings to me. And we launched Operation Brandt—to make him jealous by Alyssa bringing another date to our barbecue—and he was beside himself. But…"

Alyssa picked up the story. "I'm not proud of doing that, I know it was kind of immature but desperate times and all that. Fast forward to this week and I was completely miserable. He totally avoided me and didn't come into Tearmann. Then today I realized I was late, and I am never late. I was going to take the test first and discuss it with him after if need be, but then he showed up. We argued, and I just…I just…blurted it out."

Another stupid tear skated down her cheek, and Sophie took her now-empty wineglass and placed it on the table.

"I take it his reaction wasn't to go shopping for booties?" Kelly demanded from her perch. "What happened next?"

"He was like a robot--ice cold. He basically told me he'd never be a father and that if I chose to have the baby, he'd leave town for good." The dam broke. *Again.* Scalding tears cascaded down her cheeks.

Sophie shoved off the couch and paced around the living room. "What? Never being a father is one thing but leaving town? Leave town and have you handle this on your own? Seriously? Nick would kill him if he knew."

"Wow, did you have any idea he felt that way about kids?" Kelly asked.

"I did not. I mean, he's opening a center to help abused women and children and I know he had a tough childhood and was in the foster system." She massaged the headache brewing in her temples. "And he and Nick were both total players. He's never been in a long-term relationship, but I figured he'd be like Nick. Nick never wanted marriage or a family—until Sophie."

She smiled up at her sister-in-law. "He's a different person because of you. I thought maybe Brandt would change, too."

Sophie returned to the couch with the wine bottle. "Well, Nick didn't really change, he just learned to be vulnerable. To take a chance. Nick just froze everybody out and never really dug deep into his true feelings. He's the same guy. But it sounds like Brandt's got something deeper going on."

"Apparently." A weight settled around Alyssa's heart, and she shrugged a shoulder. Yeah, Brandt's reaction had been over the top—accusing her or manipulating him by getting pregnant was pretty extreme.

"So I'm assuming you're not pregnant?" Kelly asked.

"According to all six tests I took, that would be a big fat no. It's for the best." She reached for her wineglass. Ignored the twinge in her chest.

"Okay, well it sounds like that's good news. But what's the deal with Nick and Brandt? Would Nick really be upset if he found out? I mean you're both adults." Kelly asked.

"Nick's always been ridiculously overprotective of me since our parents died. He knows Brandt's track record with women and yeah, I doubt he'd approve. And like I mentioned, Brandt's really got no family, and Nick's the closest thing to a brother he has."

"Well, it all sounds really complicated. I'm so sorry." Kelly shook her head.

Sophie tucked her legs up beneath her and gestured with her glass. "It's definitely complicated. I figure Nick would've beat him up and then driven you guys to Vegas for a shotgun wedding. Your brother knows how important it is to you to have a big family. That you'd planned to adopt kids in addition to having your own so you could give children a big happy family like what you guys lost."

Alyssa rubbed at her eyes and shook her head to clear the foggy tendrils obscuring her brain. "I'll never know if Brandt would've reacted differently if Nick weren't his best friend."

"I mean, you wouldn't have had to sneak around. Not to be cold, but does it really matter now? It sounds like you and Brandt have diametrically opposed goals for the future." Kelly's lips pressed into a tight line.

The staccato drumbeat resumed in Alyssa's skull. She rubbed her throbbing temples, willing the pounding to cease.

"What are you going to do? Knowing Brandt never wants a family. Knowing he really never wants to get married…" Sophie asked.

Alyssa pressed a hand against her heart. "I don't know. Maybe I just projected all these feelings onto him. They never really existed except in my imagination."

Sophie scooted closer and wrapped an arm around her. "I saw the way he looks at you. He does have feelings for you, but would you be willing to sacrifice a family to be with him? Could you ever be happy knowing you gave up what you've always wanted?"

No, she couldn't be happy without starting a family.

But how could she be happy with anyone other than Brandt?

Brandt slumped on his surfboard and contemplated the shoulder-high set of waves thundering toward him. Usually, the huge swell and clean lines would make everything feel right with the world, but right now not even epic surf could boost his mood.

This morning, after another sleepless night, he'd rolled over and powered on his phone. A one word text from Alyssa popped up.

—Negative—

Dropping his head back on the pillow, he'd stared at the screen. Expecting to feel…something. Anything. Shouldn't he have felt relieved? Sad even? Instead, numbness spread through him from head to toe.

How to answer that text? *Great news, thanks* or *It's for the best* or some other worthless platitude?

So he hadn't replied. Instead, he'd grabbed his board and hit the surf. Mother Ocean usually cleared his mind. He'd hoped for inspiration or an epiphany on how to apologize to her. Nothing.

A rough slap of freezing Pacific slapped him and

knocked him off his board. Churning waves worked to keep him beneath the surface, tumbling and rolling him like a scrap of fabric in a washing machine. After a few minutes, he managed to emerge and climb back onto his board. Yeah, he needed to pay frickin' attention. The surf in California wasn't to be trifled with—not a place to be distracted.

Damn it. He'd never wanted to hurt Alyssa, which is why he tried to stay away from her. He snorted and slammed his hand against the water--yeah, he hadn't fought that hard before he'd succumbed to temptation. If only he'd had the strength to not get involved with her in the first place.

But even if he attempted a relationship with her, it was impossible because he couldn't give her what she wanted. What she deserved. If one of his parents' addiction issues had skipped him but appeared in the next generation? Or the violent tendencies? And it wasn't like he didn't have a hot temper, even if he kept it under control.

Yeah, if he'd had the spine to stay away from her, everything would be fine. He'd known it wouldn't end well. Couldn't end well. Even knowing it, he'd been unable to resist the pull of the most incredible woman he'd ever met.

And now? The situation right now was a major fucking disaster.

No consolation in being correct.

Surfing wasn't going to help today, so he paddled back into shore, not even bothering to try to catch another wave. He trudged back toward his car, tossed the surfboard into the back, and sat behind the wheel.

He pulled his phone out of the glove compartment to check if anything urgent was happening at Tearmann. Nothing. Well, besides Alyssa quitting. Yeah, and wouldn't that be fun to explain to her brother?

Before he could pull out into traffic, the phone rang with

an unfamiliar local number. A wavering voice requested Mr. Brandt.

"Kevin?"

"Umm, yeah. Any way I could get a ride with you?"

His chest tightened, imagining the worst-case scenario. "Of course, of course. Are you okay? Where are you?"

The line was silent for a moment before Kevin replied, "Yeah, yeah, I'm okay. I'm down on the corner by the main beach. Using the phone at that store."

At least the boy trusted him enough to call. "Hang tight. I'm just over at Thalia Street. I'll be there in two minutes, so don't go anywhere."

He headed north on S Coast Highway toward the popular beach situated in the middle of town. Glancing at the car's clock, he realized once again, Kevin should've been in school. Where the hell was the boy's mother? He swung into a parking space and spotted the boy leaning casually against a tree. He exhaled, the tightness in his shoulders softening. Even if he couldn't manage his own life, he could help Kevin.

Kevin peered up before dropping his gaze. "Hi, Mr. Brandt. Thanks for coming to get me."

Brandt crouched down to eye level. "Are you okay? What happened?"

"I'm okay. Just can't go to school and can't go home." His words were barely audible.

"Let's go get an ice cream, okay? You can tell me what's on your mind." Who knew when the kid had eaten last? A little sugar might soften him up and encourage him to talk.

Kevin fell in step next to him, and they headed over to Gelato Paradiso, which had the best gelato in town. Two double-scoop chocolate waffle cones in hand, they returned to the beach and sat on the edge of the pristine golden sand.

"Okay, spill it. Why aren't you in school? Where's your mom?" So much for allowing the boy to relax.

Kevin bit his lip. "I don't know. She didn't come home last night. I got scared and left really early this morning and just walked. And walked. Ended up here."

A flare of anger swelled up within him. "Didn't come home? Has this happened before?"

"Um…she was out with some guy she met."

"Like a date?" And left a nine-year-old boy alone. Brandt gritted his teeth.

"Yeah. He came up on a motorcycle, and it was really loud. She ran out and told me to watch TV, but our cable got turned off, so there was nothing to watch."

Brandt exhaled a slow, steadying breath. "Your mom has a job, right?"

"Kind of. Well, not right now. She's had jobs. Waitressing, cooking, and some office stuff. They don't last long…" Kevin trailed off and stared down at his gelato.

"How about this? Finish your cone, and I'll drive you home and talk to your mom. She's probably back now and worried about you." Damn well better be.

Kevin shrugged a bony shoulder. "Sure, but I doubt it."

They headed to the car, and he buckled Kevin in. Noticed the frayed shorts, dirty T-shirt, and ancient flip-flops. At least he had shoes on today.

Kevin gave him an address on the southeast side of town. They ended up in a neighborhood that didn't look too bad. Hell, nothing in Laguna was scary to look at, not like some parts of Los Angeles. The boy pointed to a worn-down single-story cottage with patchy brown grass dotting a pitiful excuse for a front yard.

When he parked, Kevin led him around back to a smaller building, about the size of a garden shed. They both lived there? And his mother entertained men with Kevin in that house. He ground his molars and struggled for calm.

A skinny woman with mousy brown hair and last night's

makeup barked when they entered the filthy room. "Kevin, where've you been?"

The kid shrugged again.

She yanked Kevin toward her. "Who are you? What are you doing with my kid?" Her bloodshot gaze raked over him, taking in his board shorts and faded T-shirt.

"What if I'm from his school? Or from social services checking on reports of a regularly absent student?" Or just a man who recognizes the signs of a neglected child.

Her smeared, raccoon eyes sharpened. "You aren't from the school. Who are you?"

"My name is Brandt Dempsey. Kevin's safe with me. But he should be in school, and he is too young to be left alone all night. Look, I might be able to help you both, but we need to talk."

"We don't need help. We're just fine. You stay away from my kid. Get out of here." Her voice grew shrill.

"Mom, he's cool—" Kevin broke off when she dug her fingers into his flesh.

Brandt forced himself to smile at the boy and speak in a neutral tone. "Kevin, go outside for a minute. Don't go anywhere. Your mom and I are going to have a little talk. Okay?"

Kevin slid out from his mother's grasp and scampered out the front door.

"You have no business—"

Brandt prayed for patience. "Look, lady, I saw the bruises he had. He's not going to school. If you don't want me to call social services right now and have him taken into foster care, you'll listen to what I have to say."

Her jaw clamped shut, and she crossed her skinny arms across her narrow chest. "Fine. Go ahead."

"Look, I can help you guys. Help you find a job and a

bigger apartment. Make sure he's in school." Give him a chance.

Her eyes widened. "Why do you care? What's in it for you? You have no idea how hard I work to put food on the—"

He held up a hand. "Listen to me. I get it. I know it's tough. I've got a place I'm building, a center where you can get some help getting a better job or training or whatever you need. Where you're safe, where your boy has a better chance."

"Place?"

"What's your name?" Hell, he didn't even know her name. Was she an alcoholic? Or worse? Judging by the empty wine bottles squatting next to a sink overflowing with food-caked dishes, she wasn't exactly a stellar housekeeper.

Her stance softened slightly. "Kitty. Kitty Concannon. Go on. I'm listening."

"Kitty, it's called Tearmann House, and it's for women and kids who need a place to get back on their feet, some assistance outside the system. But if you're an addict—"

She glared at him. "I'm not a damn addict. His shithead of a father was a junkie and took off years ago. It's been me trying to keep him in clothes and school and food and…"

He gestured around the pitiful excuse for a home. "What about the bruises? What about the bottles?"

"I like my wine, but I'm no drunk. The last guy I dated was one, and he grabbed Kevin. I dumped him for putting marks on my boy. I love my kid." Her eyes filled, but some people could cry on cue.

"Are you sure?" He stepped closer, searching her face. Although this woman didn't appear to be abused or an abuser, she could be a skillful liar.

She crossed one finger across her chest. "I swear. It's just so hard to get ahead, and a little wine at night helps me deal.

I can work, though. I've got a high school degree. Just all the jobs are so shitty, don't make enough to pay rent, feed him…"

He strode to the messy counter and found a pencil and a small notepad. He scratched down his number and thrust the sheet of paper at her. "Take this. Call me tomorrow, and I'll coordinate a meeting with one of my employees to help you get some training, some job prep, and some new clothes if needed. Just make sure Kevin's in school tomorrow and every day."

She accepted the paper and glanced down. "Why are you doing this? You don't know me. This doesn't make sense."

He massaged the tight muscles on the back of his neck. "Consider me a good Samaritan. I see potential in your son. He's smart. He deserves a chance at a good education, a chance to be a kid."

She folded the piece of paper and stuffed it in her back pocket. "Okay, I'll call tomorrow."

Satisfied he'd done all he could, he went outside, where Kevin sat on the back porch of the front house. He joined him on the stoop.

This kid tugged at him. "You're a smart kid, aren't you?"

"Math's okay." He nibbled on his cuticle.

He would help this boy who was like a mirror from his past. "Math was my favorite too. Look, I'm going to help your mom find work. You guys can come stay at Tearmann House for a while. But I need you to go to school. Get good grades. Education is important."

Kevin's root-beer eyes grew crafty. "Will it get me a sweet car like what you drive?"

Brandt laughed, his heart warming. "It's a great start."

"I want a Corvette just like yours. And I want to surf all day."

Brandt patted Kevin on the back. "Well, to do that, you've

got to earn it. Nobody gives you the lifestyle without work. But you can do whatever you want if you work hard."

Kevin's cheeks flushed. "You think?"

"I know. If I can do it, so can you." A rusty gear shifted in Brandt's chest, unlocking something.

If he truly believed Kevin could have a normal life, why couldn't he accept that he could too? If Kevin was innocent of the sins of his deadbeat dad, wasn't he?

Despite his upbringing, he had turned out all right. Despite his parents being low-life addicts and his dad a vicious criminal. Despite all of it, he'd built a life for himself.

On his own. His "Uncle John" had given him a chance, and that's what he'd do for Kevin. Maybe fate didn't control it all. Maybe there wasn't a predetermined ending. Maybe he was predisposed to be a certain way, but he'd overcome it. Chosen a different path.

If he could beat the odds and become a successful entrepreneur, could he apply the same principles to becoming a good enough man to deserve Alyssa? Or at least spend a lifetime trying?

Because he chose Alyssa. Nothing mattered without her. The few weeks they'd spent together had been the most alive he'd ever been.

He shot to his feet. He needed to see her. To apologize. He'd brave Nick's wrath, he'd go public, and he'd do whatever it took to be with her as a true partner. Anything to win her back.

He couldn't imagine his life without her. He'd convince her to marry him. He'd have some groveling to do after how much of a dick he'd been when she'd shared she might be pregnant.

He hesitated––he still wasn't sure about the kid thing. At least his own children. He liked kids. But what if they were more like his parents? Maybe they could compromise and adopt a bunch of kids.

"Mr. Brandt?" Kevin tilted his head to one side.

"I've got to go, Kevin, but it's all going to be okay. Just go to school tomorrow." He ruffled the boy's hair and hightailed it back to his car.

Time to stop being such a coward and put his heart on the line. Serve his heart to Alyssa. If she even wanted it anymore.

lyssa poured another huge mug of coffee, praying it eliminated the rest of her lingering headache the aspirin had failed to address. She massaged her aching temples. Last night's wine-and-chocolate binge, though absolutely crucial to maintain her sanity, wasn't exactly the fuel of champions.

They'd drunk, dissected, and analyzed her dilemma until three a.m. when exhaustion finally claimed them. Both Kelly and Sophie stayed overnight. Kelly drove back to San Diego bright and early, and Sophie returned home after a hit of caffeine. Now she was alone, and her condo was quiet as a tomb.

Radio silence from Brandt. Big surprise. But did she even want to hear from him?

She settled onto the couch and sipped her coffee. At least now her eyes were dry. What a miracle. The waterfall of tears seemed endless, but everything was finite, right?

Although her yoga practice taught her to live in the present moment, the present moment sucked. She'd cleared most of her other projects over the next month for Tearmann House, so burying herself in work wasn't an option at least for today. A day off with no plan was a dangerous recipe for brooding.

Could she shift into autopilot by baking some muffins? No, she wouldn't be able to eat them. Go to yoga? No way. Class could stir up the jumbled emotions she'd rather suppress for now. The beach? Maybe. Digging her toes into the sand and watching the ebb and flow of the ocean might be her best bet to begin healing her fractured heart.

But first, she'd finish her coffee and will away the headache from hell. She closed her eyes and practiced extending her inhales and exhales. Difficult to conjure peace and quiet with a troupe of flamenco dancers inside her skull.

Someone banged on her front door. Her eyes flew open, and her heart kicked in her chest. Who would be at the door in the middle of the afternoon? She hadn't indulged in any retail therapy lately and wasn't expecting any deliveries. Little girls selling cookies, random survey takers, and maga-zine hawkers could move along to her neighbors, thank you very much.

She nestled farther into the couch cushions. *Please go away, whoever you are.*

The hammering continued. No such luck.

"Alyssa, I know you're in there," Brandt called through the solid wood door.

Her heart soared momentarily and then tumbled. "Go away."

He'd give up and slink off, right? It wasn't as if he had a track record for sticking around.

"Alyssa, please. Give me a few minutes. I've got to talk to you." His voice sounded different, more gravelly.

Why was he here now? She couldn't survive another horrible scene like yesterday morning. Was it only yesterday? "There's nothing to discuss. Go away."

He rattled the doorknob. "Damn it, Alyssa. Open this door or I'll kick it in, and I'd really rather not do that."

Kick the door in? Seriously? "Fine. Hold on."

She surged to her feet, willing her churning belly to calm. She rubbed her chest, her heart a gaping wound. She yanked the door open and steeled herself. "What do you want?"

"Hi." His sea-blue eyes were warm when they met hers, his square jaw shadowed with dark stubble.

Of course, he had to look positively delicious.

She crossed her arms across her threadbare sweatshirt and cursed her decision not to wash her face or brush her hair. So much for looking her best and making him suffer. "You have five minutes. Talk."

"Can we sit down? Please?" He reached out one strong hand.

"Fine. Don't touch me, though." She retreated a step— ignore that sinewy forearm— marched to the sofa and huddled into the cushions.

When he started to join her, she snapped and waved him away. "Give me some space. Sit over there." No way could she share the couch where they'd created so many hot memories.

He nodded and sat facing her on the edge of the armchair. He rubbed his hand across his square chin and gazed down for a moment, dark lashes shielding his eyes.

"I don't know where to start..." A tremor cracked his usually rich voice.

Surprised, she considered his expression. The glacier-faced stranger from yesterday was nowhere to be seen. Today's Brandt looked younger than usual, vulnerable even. Could she trust him?

More to the point: could she trust herself? She held up three fingers. "Three and a half minutes."

"Okay, I'll start with an apology. I'm so sorry about everything I said. I didn't mean any of it. I just freaked out and I was wrong."

"Oh, you meant it all right. I saw you. I heard you. You made it crystal clear what you thought of me." You punched a hole through my heart.

He started to rise from the chair.

She pointed a finger at him. "Stay over there." Every muscle in her body clenched in an effort to remain calm. To appear calm anyway.

He sank back onto the edge of the chair and rubbed his face with his hands. "Alyssa, I'm so sorry. Of course I trust you. But everything about having children is…complicated. I meant what I said that I should never have children…"

She sucked in a breath. "Then why are you here? What's the point?"

"Because you matter. Because I want to make things right between us." Sincerity gleamed in his eyes. "Hear me out. I've never told anyone what I'm about to tell you. Whatever you do after that is up to you. But I have a really good reason for why I swore I'd never have kids."

She gripped her coffee mug so tight it was a miracle it didn't disintegrate in her hands. "If this is all some misguided effort to get me to finish at Tearmann House, you can forget—"

He raked his fingers through his hair. "Of course it's not about Tearmann House. Please just let me explain."

"Fine." She struggled to breathe regularly.

"My parents were both addicts. I'm talking living in shit-holes, hard drugs, stealing, and doing anything to rustle up cash for the next drink or hit." He paused and looked down at his hands. "It's all I knew. I was a nuisance. A mouth to feed. They made damn sure I knew they wished I'd never been born."

"Brandt, you don't know that—" The ice encasing her heart began to thaw.

"Yes, I do. They told me." He hesitated, then lifted his head and pierced her with his now bleak gaze. "My dad used his fists or his belt, and my mom preferred to slap and pinch."

Righteous anger flooded her veins. "Brandt—"

He held up a hand. "Anyway, the drugs eventually killed them. I ended up in some foster homes that weren't much better. I ran away a few times and finally it stuck."

She rose from the couch and approached him, wanting to help wipe away the desolation shadowing his face. This time, he retreated. He stood and paced to the fireplace on the other side of the room. He dropped one hand against the mantle, the lines of his body rigid.

"Let me finish. I lucked out and met my now-honorary uncle John, who worked at a crappy little jeweler. He caught me dumpster-diving behind his store and long story short, gave me a job and got me back into school. If it weren't for him, I'm sure I'd be dead or in prison right now."

Her heart squeezed for the lost little boy he'd been, for the lost little boy who still resided within him. "Brandt, it's not your fault. You were a child. You can't choose your parents. You're amazing—look at all you've accomplished, all you've done, all the good you do in the world..."

He pivoted to face her, hands clenched and eyes aflame. "I swore I'd never have kids because addiction is hereditary. Maybe violent tendencies and evil are too. I'd never be able to live with myself."

"You created who you are today. I don't believe in pedigrees or being fated by who your parents are. You're successful and compassionate, and you're definitely not a violent addict."

He shook his head and turned back toward the hearth. "I

get it on one level, but what if? What if I helped create a child who was a monster? My parents were monsters. I've never wanted to risk it. You've got to understand."

"But what if? Come on, you are creating a sanctuary for kids who come from tough situations. Will you tell all of them not to have kids because they've been dealt a crappy hand?"

"Of course not…" He angled back toward her.

"Exactly. Why judge yourself more harshly?"

He scrubbed his hands across his face. "I did realize that. I met a boy who showed me he's got potential, despite a deadbeat dad and not-great mom. But…"

Her heart softened knowing his freak-out had roots in things that had nothing to do with her. "But nothing. Your reaction makes more sense now. Do you still feel that way?"

He shrugged one broad shoulder. "I created Tearmann House for the kids. I want to help as many as I can."

"You are helping." She clasped her hands together and squeezed tight. "But you made it clear you don't want to be with me, so while I appreciate you explaining your reasons, it doesn't change things with us."

He took two long strides toward her. "Alyssa, hear me out. I—"

"No, it's still too painful." She held up a hand to halt his progress. "I can't work with you anymore. Maybe one day, but for now I can't see you."

"Alyssa." He reached for her hands. She tried to tug them away, but he tightened his hold.

"You broke my heart. Don't you understand that?" A tear streamed down her face. Why was he torturing her?

He brushed the tear away with his thumb. "Please don't cry. Look at me."

She met his gaze, no longer hiding her hurt, her love, her

heart. Perhaps he'd understand the pain and leave her to heal. Alone.

"Alyssa." He cupped her jaw. "I've been such an idiot. I'm not worthy of you, but I want to try if you'll give me a chance."

A flicker of hope ignited in her chest. But she didn't trust her voice to reply.

His gaze remained unwavering. "I want us to go talk to Nick. Tonight."

"Talk to Nick?" Her jaw dropped.

"Yes, talk to Nick. We'll go talk to Nick tonight." His jaw was determined, and his eyes alight with passion.

Her pulse kicked up in her veins. "And tell him what?"

"Tell him that I love you. I love every single thing about you—your strength, your kindness, your smartass sense of humor, your stubbornness. I love it all." Tenderness shone in the cerulean depths of his eyes.

Her breath caught in her throat. "What did you say?"

"I said 'I love you.' Will you give me a chance? Take a shot at a real relationship with me? Am I too late?" His brow creased.

She launched herself at him in a burst of tears and laughter and wound her arms around his neck. "Yes, yes, yes. I love you, Brandt. Everything about you too."

He crushed his mouth to hers and tugged her down to the couch, and she landed on top of him. His large hands molded her against every inch of his lean, muscular frame. His tongue tangled and danced with hers, sending shivers down her spine. He pulled back and planted featherlight kisses along her jaw and cheeks, stroked the stray strands escaping her messy bun away from her face.

"Wait." She pressed her forearms into his sculpted pecs, creating some distance. She needed to see his face, needed to ask one more question before she could surrender. The muscles in her belly clenched.

"Wait for what? It's been too long since I've held you. And this couch brings back some hot memories." He winked.

The fluttering in her stomach increased to a roiling ache. "No, wait. We still need to talk about kids. Kids are still a deal breaker for me."

He closed his eyes and pressed his forehead up against hers. He drew in a ragged breath. Sighed it out.

Frost began to wrap its tendrils around her heart again.

He opened his eyes. "What if we adopt? We can adopt a football team if you want. That would be so much safer—"

She brushed a lock of dark hair away from his forehead. "You admitted yourself that the kids you helped aren't to blame and neither are you. Forget safe. I want a child with you, Brandt. Our baby. We'd be amazing parents, and that's what matters. We'd love our child no matter what, right? And I'd love to adopt too. I do want a football team. A loud, boisterous house full of love."

His eyes drifted shut. "I just don't know—"

"What if we went and talked to a counselor? You could go alone, and work on stuff and we could go together. We could talk it over with someone. Take some time to process all of it and get used to the idea. We don't have to have a child tomorrow, but I think it would help for a professional to reassure you too."

Brandt cracked open one eye. "You really want me to go to a shrink?"

She gathered her courage and swallowed the nerves dancing in her belly. "Look, I'm going to share something with you that most people don't know about. It might help you understand why I think therapy is so great and also help you understand more about Nick's uber-protectiveness. Why he's so over-the-top determined to protect me."

Brandt loved her, so her past wouldn't change that. Would it?

A line formed between his dark brows. "I didn't mean to say that therapy is bad."

She pressed one finger against his perfect chiseled mouth. "Now it's your turn to listen. Do you remember when you helped me with those bullies all those years ago? When I almost fell down the stairs at the beach?"

His brows drew together, and he nodded.

"Well, part of why I was so weak was I hadn't eaten for more than a day. I was anorexic in high school, so Nick thinks I'm fragile. He's worried the wrong man or wrong situation will trigger a relapse." Her breath whooshed out.

Brandt reached up and stroked his fingers lightly down her cheek. "Oh, babe, I'm so sorry. What happened?"

"Well, after our parents died, I ended up in a fancy boarding school so I could be near Nick in New York. The girls there were horrible." She shuddered at the memory of the cruel clique. "I let their bullying and my loneliness get the better of me. They didn't eat, so I followed along to fit in. Then I couldn't stop. I think I felt so abandoned when my parents died, and it was just Nick and me. Food became a mechanism where I felt like I had some control."

She shrugged. "It took a lot of therapy, even an in-hospital program and I've been fine for years. Nick somehow blamed himself for not being able to help me more and now I think he worries that if my heart were broken again, I'd regress or something."

"Alyssa, I'm so sorry. I hope I haven't pushed you in that direction." His gaze was searching.

"No, you wounded my heart, but I didn't relapse. I just couldn't eat because I was so upset. But being alone at school in my teenage years and Nick and I having no other relatives is why it's so important to me to have a large family. I've always dreamed of being surrounded by people I can love and who love me."

He cradled her jaw in his hand. "Thank you for sharing with me. I get it. I guess I'm not the only one with scars. I'll definitely go talk to someone––by myself and with you. I'll do whatever I can to make you happy. Can you be patient with me because you may have noticed that spilling my feelings isn't exactly one of my strong points."

She laughed, the last vestige of chill seeping away as her heart heated. It wasn't a perfect answer, but all she wanted was a chance. A chance to show him his fears were unfounded, and they could create their own destiny together.

"That's perfect. You're worth waiting for." She pressed a soft kiss on his lips and allowed her body to relax against his.

She lifted her head. "Are you serious about going to tell Nick tonight? So soon?"

"It's not soon. It's late. I should have gone with you to the airport when you asked me. We should have told them together then. So, now I'm ready. I'm going to tell him I love you and we're getting married, and he can just deal with it."

Alyssa gasped and her heart knocked against her ribs. *Married?*

He arched a dark brow at her, a hint of a smile quirking his lips up at the corners. "What?"

"Would you mind repeating that?" Her pulse hammered in her throat.

He grinned now, teasing her. "It's not too soon. I—"

"That's not what I meant." She fisted her hands in his silky hair and tugged.

He wrapped his arms around her and pressed her closer against him. "Married, when we get married. You started it when you caught the damn bouquet. Now you're stuck with me. You're mine––do you think I'd ever let you go?"

Nose to nose now, joy bubbled through her. "Um, haven't you forgotten something?"

"Forgotten what?" He stroked his large hands down her back, cupped her bottom, and squeezed.

She rocked her hips against him, savoring the friction from the steel-hard erection in his shorts. "Isn't it customary to ask someone to marry you as opposed to dropping it casually into conversation?"

Brandt growled, rolled, and lifted her up to sit on the couch. "See? I'm an idiot."

He nudged her thighs apart and knelt between her legs. He caught her hands in his warm ones. "Alyssa Morgan, love of my life, will you marry me and make me the happiest man on earth for the rest of our lives?"

Happiness sparkled through her, and she squeezed her eyes shut, savoring the warmth radiating from her heart.

"Alyssa? Just say yes. I don't have a ring, but we'll go buy you one tomorrow—anything you want."

Her lips curved upward. "Oh, well, if you're going to put a ring on it…yes, absolutely yes."

He laughed softly. "Let's make it official in the spot where you first seduced me."

In one quick move, he'd wrapped her legs around him and shifted them onto the couch together.

"Me? Seduce you?" She straddled him and tightened her thighs around him. "Let's see if I remember exactly how."

Together, they ripped his T-shirt off, and she sighed with pleasure looking down at the handsome, incredible man beneath her. She stroked her hands along his sculpted torso, trailing her fingers across his six-pack abs, stopping to tug the drawstring on his board shorts.

He reached for her, but she pushed him back into the cushions, savoring the feminine energy coursing through her veins. He was hers, and she wanted to take control.

"Alyssa—" His breath hissed out when she rocked her center against him.

She pressed two fingers to his lips and leaned down to kiss his broad chest. "Shhh…just lie back and enjoy."

She took her time and tasted, caressed, and kissed until she reached the waistband of his shorts. Gently peeled it open to reveal smooth velvety skin before she lowered her head and slid her mouth over him. His hips jerked upward, and his hands buried themselves in her hair. His groans and harsh breathing spurred her on, each rough outburst shooting sparks of heat directly to her center.

She lifted her gaze and smiled at him, thrilled at the power she had to please him. Excited to find how much giving to him turned her on.

"No more. Come here. Now." He growled low in his throat. Dragged her up along his body. "Fuck, condom."

She moaned. "Hurry."

His nostrils flared, his fingers digging into her hips. "Wallet. Back pocket. Give me a second?"

"Hurry." She repeated and caught her lower lip in her teeth.

"These. Off. Now." He tugged at her sweats, and they struggled to get rid of them. She managed to shove off one pant leg, too impatient to do more. He grabbed a condom from his wallet, rolled it on in record time, and inch by inch, she took him inside her.

"Fuck, Alyssa." He held her still. "You feel incredible. So tight. So hot. So perfect for me. I love you." His voice was raw, rough.

His gaze burned into her, full of love and passion and heat. "I'm yours."

"And I'm yours. I love you Brandt Dempsey." She began to move.

He caught her hands and intertwined his fingers with

hers, never breaking their gaze. The feel of him inside her, the knowledge that he was finally hers, spurred her on until they came apart in long waves of pleasure, together.

MUCH LATER, they forced themselves to leave the safety of the couch to shower and prepare for what promised to be a battle with Nick. While she meticulously applied some makeup and dried her hair, Brandt called Nick to let him know they were heading over in about an hour.

He set the phone down, slid his arms around her, and pulled her back against his hard, hot front. He nuzzled her neck, sending tingles down her spine. She leaned against him for a moment.

"If we're going to make it over there tonight, we should get going." A hint of nerves fluttered in her belly. Nick wasn't going to be easy to convince.

"True." With one last kiss on the sensitive skin on her neck, he stepped back. "Let's swing by my place so I can change clothes.

They climbed into his Range Rover and fastened their seat belts. With one hand clasping hers, he navigated back to his gorgeous house on the hill. When he ran into the house to change, she waited inside the car, gathering her composure for their upcoming discussion with her brother.

He emerged moments later looking scrumptious in dark jeans and a collared white shirt. He rejoined her in the truck and started to turn on the engine.

A frisson of nerves jolted through her. "Wait."

He turned to face her; his gaze wary. "Wait? You aren't having second thoughts, are you? Like realizing I'm not worthy of you?"

"No, of course not." She linked her fingers with his and

squeezed. "I'm just a little worried about Nick's initial reaction." Maybe a lot worried.

He shifted and gathered her in his arms, hugging her as close as the confines of the front seat allowed. "Look, he'll probably punch me, and I'll take it. But eventually, Nick will accept us. He has to." He shifted back to the driver's side and turned on the engine. "Let's do this."

Reassured, she settled back into the buttery leather seat. A few minutes later, he pulled up the long drive and parked behind Nick's car.

Alyssa took a fortifying breath. "What did you tell him anyway?"

"I just let him think it was about Tearmann House. Figured we'd do this in person." He shrugged.

She placed her hand on his muscular, denim-clad thigh. "You should let me tell Nick. He'll handle it better coming from me."

He shook his head. "Forget it. I'll tell him. I'm not hiding anymore."

"Let's tell him together. I'll let you start. And Sophie's on our side. Well, she was…" Oh crap.

Brandt's eyebrows shot up to his hairline. "Shit, she knows about—"

"Well, yesterday she called right after I left Tearmann House. I was upset, and she insisted on driving me down to Dana Point. She bought the tests, and then she stayed over at my house last night."

"So now she hates my guts and honestly, after the night at the barbecue? I'm more worried about her kicking my ass than Nick."

Alyssa giggled. "Yeah, she was scary Principal Sophie. She doesn't hate you, but…let's just say she just doesn't think we'd be right together if you don't want kids. I think once you tell them we're together, she'll be on our side. She's a huge romantic."

He gripped the steering wheel, his knuckles white with tension. "This is all my fault, dammit—"

"Look, it's all in the past. There are no secrets now. Let's deal with tonight and then one day at a time. Nick will come around." If only her words sounded more like a statement than a question.

Her pulse was thrumming in her ears, her nerves bubbling at a fever pitch. Despite her bravado and pep talk for Brandt, she hated confrontation, and tonight promised to be an epic one.

Brandt caught her shoulders and captured her mouth in a quick hot kiss. "It's going to be fine, don't worry. Let's do this."

$\mathcal{B}$randt kept Alyssa's hand gripped in his and willed the sweat prickling between his shoulder blades to disappear. Alyssa tapped on the door twice before opening it and entering Nick and Sophie's house.

"We're in the kitchen. C'mon back," Sophie called.

"Here goes nothing." Brandt squeezed her hand as they walked into the kitchen together.

His pulse thundered through his veins, but he'd be damned if he'd let Nick see his nervousness. The firm grip of Alyssa's slender fingers intertwined with his bolstered his courage. Hell, if he could propose, agree to go to a therapist, and discuss babies, he could handle Nick's temper.

Although he didn't want to alienate his best friend nor cause a wedge between Alyssa and her brother, now that Alyssa was his, he wasn't letting her go. Yeah, he was a selfish bastard, so what?

Sophie's big blue eyes rounded comically when they entered the room holding hands. Her incredulous gaze swung between him and Alyssa. He shrugged and attempted a smile.

"Hey, guys, what's going on? Want a beer?" Nick's voice echoed from inside the enormous refrigerator. Shoving it closed, he turned toward them with a bottle of microbrew in his hand. His mouth dropped open when he focused in on their joined hands.

"What the—" His face suffused with red.

Time to lay his cards on the table. "Nick, we need to talk to you—" Brandt began.

Nick slammed his unopened beer onto the kitchen island and stalked toward them. "We? What the hell is going on?"

Alyssa held up a hand. "Nick, you need to take a breath and listen."

"Nick, wait a minute and give them a chance to explain—" Sophie grabbed his arm.

His head snapped toward his wife. "You knew about this?"

Sophie shook her head. "Not really but remember this is your little sister and your best friend."

Nick hissed. "Yeah, that's the fucking problem. My only sister and the guy who has never been in a relationship before holding hands in my goddamn kitchen."

"Sweetie, you'd never been in a committed relationship before me." Sophie pressed one hand to Nick's chest.

"It's not the same." Nick pointed at him, pivoted, and stalked toward the patio. "You. Outside. Now."

Brandt recognized the fury in Nick's eyes. Understood it. Yeah, Nick wasn't ready to listen to any of them right now. The time for talking would have to wait.

"Nick, just calm down and let's all sit down. We can explain everything—" Alyssa's voice was soothing.

"Not you. Him. You stay in here." He shoved the French doors open.

Brandt gently loosened Alyssa's death grip on his hand. "It'll be okay." As long as Nick didn't kill him first.

He followed Nick outside and scanned the deck for

weapons. No barbecue or gardening tools appeared to be within reach, so at least he wouldn't get skewered. Good thing because Nick's expression resembled the killers on those nighttime crime dramas.

Nick planted his feet, his fists clenched, his eyes flinty. "Give me one reason why I shouldn't rip you apart."

Brandt let out a harsh breath and held up his hands. "Look, I know you're pissed now, but we—"

"Pissed doesn't begin to describe it. You've got thirty seconds, and then I'm kicking your ass."

"It all started at the wedding…" He winced. *Shit*. No way could he tell Nick his baby sister had propositioned him to a two-week sex fest.

Nick's expression darkened, and he moved a step closer. "The wedding? My wedding where I asked you to protect her? I asked you to look out for her. To keep the players away from her. Fuck, man, you're the biggest player of them all. That wedding?"

Brandt cleared his throat. "Look, I'm in love with Alyssa, and we—"

"Love? Is that how you got my sister to sleep with you? Told her you loved her? You've never screwed the same woman twice, and you took advantage of my sister?" Nick lunged and landed a right hook to his nose.

He pressed a hand to his face and a warm spurt of blood trickled down his cheek. Brandt accepted the sharp pain. He deserved it––if the situation were reversed and Sophie had been his little sister––he would do the same thing.

When Nick followed with a solid punch to his gut, he shoved him away. Not *that* much pain. "I deserved the first punch, but no more. Will you just listen to me for one goddamn minute?"

Nick paused, panting, his fists still raised and ready.

"Listen. To. Me. Alyssa isn't a child. She's a woman, and she knows what she's doing. We both do."

Nick lowered his hands and shook his head. "You don't understand--she seems so strong, but you don't really know her—inside she's fragile. She's not like other women. She's—"

"Bullshit. She's anything but fragile. She's the bravest, strongest, kindest woman I've ever met. I love her. Everything about her. She told me about school and her issues. You've got to stop seeing her through the lens of the past and see her for who she is now.

"She accepts me for who I am—all of it. I accept her too. You and I agree I'm not good enough for her. Nobody is. But I'll be damned if you stand in my way of spending the rest of my life showing her she's the most incredible woman on the planet and proving how much I love her."

Screw Nick. Screw them all. He didn't deserve Alyssa, but damn it, she loved him. And no way in hell would he let her go now. He'd do all the therapy. Whatever it took.

Nick's eyes widened. "The rest of your life? Are you saying—"

"Yeah, I'm marrying your sister, and I hope to God you don't ruin it all by being a dick. She'd die without you in her life and…" He closed his eyes for a moment and dug deep. "And damn it, you're my brother too, and my life wouldn't be the same without you in it. Please don't stand in our way."

Nick's jaw dropped. Brandt couldn't blame him, as it was hands down the longest speech he'd ever given, except for that commencement address at USC and that had been scripted. And he was pretty sure he'd never said "please" to Nick for any reason whatsoever.

"You really love her." Nick's quiet words weren't a question or a threat.

Brandt's heart tightened in his chest. "More than the

world. I know you're pissed and shocked, but can you give us a chance to prove I can make her happy?"

Nick rubbed the scruff on his jaw and considered him. "Yeah, I will. It may take me a while to get used to it though. And if you hurt her, I'll kill you. Understand?"

The tension drained from Brandt's shoulders. "I'll let you."

"Do I need to call nine-one-one, or is it safe to come out there now?" Sophie called from where she and Alyssa stood framed in the doorway.

Nick snickered. "Nah, but Brandt probably needs an ice pack."

"Nick, was that really necessary?" Sophie marched outside--yeah, the Principal was back in the building.

"Yes." Nick and Brandt answered simultaneously.

Alyssa rushed over to his side and stroked his cheek "You're bleeding. Nick, you jerk. You didn't have to hit him."

Brandt hugged her tight into his side, basking in her concern. "It's fine. He punches with the power of an angry toddler. Just a scratch."

Sophie and Alyssa looked at each other and shook their heads.

"You two are children." Sophie rolled her eyes and grabbed Nick's arm. "Get inside. I'm popping the bottle of Dom Perignon we were saving for a special occasion. I think this qualifies."

Alyssa gazed up at him, her smoky blue eyes shining with love. He lowered his head to kiss her, but she stopped him. "Let's get rid of the blood first, please. Then I'm going to sit on your lap, and we'll kiss in front of my brother, just because he deserves it."

Brandt laughed. "You like to tempt fate. As long as we're not in striking distance. I'm already going to have a black eye."

Hand in hand, they followed Nick and Sophie back into the house. He hadn't been kidding--his nose hurt like hell--but the worst was over. Back in the kitchen, they popped the champagne, and despite Nick's occasional measuring glances, Brandt's heart was full. Sometimes true family had nothing to do with blood and everything to do with choice. He and Nick were going to be okay but better than that?

He'd been lucky enough to be chosen by the woman of his dreams. He'd gotten the girl and he couldn't wait for the whole world to know Alyssa Morgan would be his wife.

"Toast, toast." Alyssa tapped her champagne flute. She smiled as she gazed at the crowd gathered in the Tearmann House recreation room for the grand-opening party. A muscular arm slid around her waist and hugged her back against a solid chest.

"I think everyone's already toasting, babe," Brandt murmured in her ear. "We could always sneak away to the conference room for old time's sake?"

She elbowed him in his six-pack. "Not a chance. I've got some things to say, and everyone's going to listen."

He waggled his eyebrows. "I love it when you get forceful with me. Are you sure we can't head back to the conference room…"

"No, now behave. At least for a little while." She angled back toward the crowd. "Listen up." She shouted and finally everyone shifted their attention to where she and Brandt stood.

She smiled at Kevin, Brandt's little friend, dressed in a button-down shirt and pressed shorts. His mother was with him, looking relaxed and content. Kevin waved at them, happiness sparkling in his big brown eyes. They were the first official "family members" at Tearmann House.

Joy bubbled through her system. "Thanks so much for sharing this special day with us. My fiancé dreamed of opening a center where those who weren't welcome elsewhere, who were ignored by the system, or who just needed a helping hand to create a better life for themselves had a place to go. Tearmann means safe haven in Gaelic. And that's what Brandt Dempsey's vision, dedication, and hard work—"

"And boatloads of cash," Nick shouted from the back corner where he was hanging out with Sophie, Kelly, and Christian.

"And lots of money, yes. But that's what's so amazing about my fiancé. He came from a rough childhood, didn't have parents or any advantages, and through hard work and a little luck, made boatloads of money, as my lovely brother so aptly put it. He funded every dime of this center.

"But money is only part of it. What's really important, what will make Tearmann House a true success, is the heart behind it all. A place where people can come and have the chance to turn things around. Where everyone can feel part of a family, a community. I couldn't be more proud to be a part of it. Thanks to my brother, Nick Morgan, for his fantastic design. Let's all give a hand to Brandt Dempsey and an incredible future for Tearmann House."

Applause thundered through the room, echoing off the high ceiling. Cheers and hoots filled the space and Alyssa turned and wrapped her arms around Brandt. "Babe, you did it."

Brandt hugged her tight, burying his face in her hair. "We did it. I couldn't have done it without you and Nick. Thank you for believing in me. I love you so much."

"I love you too." She shifted back and pressed a long,

lingering kiss on his mouth. "Let's go hang with the family and Kelly. I'm so glad she could make it up today."

Now Nick and Brandt weren't just best friends, they were soon to be brothers, for real. And Sophie was fast becoming the same for her––best friend and sister. Alyssa's heart burst with happiness.

Brandt kept her tucked close into his side and together they crossed the room. When they reached the small group, Nick was chatting with Brandt's Uncle John, who had driven down from L.A. for the opening celebration.

But the very interesting thing was Christian stood with his arms folded across his broad chest, his green-gold eyes laser-focused on Kelly, who was huddled close to Sophie, whispering. His chiseled jaw was tight, his posture military straight, despite having left the Army and opening Vines, a local wine bar. He was watching Kelly like he couldn't tear his gaze away.

Hmm…interesting. Kelly had recently dumped her boyfriend and Christian was single. Nick and Brandt loved the guy and Sophie had mentioned when Kelly first saw Christian, she'd totally thought he was hot.

Kelly excused herself and sauntered to the bar and Christian tracked her every step. Very interesting.

Maybe at her and Brandt's wedding, she'd toss her bouquet to Kelly, just like Sophie had with her. Wouldn't it be fascinating to see how Mr. Brooding Military Man handled it.

READY FOR KELLY **and Christian's story?**

A SMALL TOWN Grumpy Sunshine Contemporary Romance
When Christian Wolfe returns to Laguna Beach after four

tours in the Middle East, he carries hidden scars. He buys a wine bar and vows to keep his life simple and his PTSD secret. When stunning Kelly Prescott and her red stilettos saunter into town, something about the brainy beauty makes him want to tell her everything - and that's a risk he just can't take. Can he?

Kelly escaped her father's cutthroat corporate law firm and left behind both family and courtroom drama, to move to Laguna. Her new role as general counsel for a veterans' nonprofit fulfills her need to make a difference. But she didn't bargain on meeting a brooding war hero who tugs on her heartstrings. Christian is sexy and smart, and Kelly can't resist the challenge of trying to bring a little bit of sunshine to the grumpy ex-soldier. But can she convince him to let her in?

WANT A **FREE** SHORT STORY? Snap up *Perfect Rivals*, the Prequel to my spin-off California Suits series and stay up to date with new releases, book signings and events, and receive exclusive giveaways and sneak peeks, by signing up for my monthly newsletter: https://clairemarti.com/newsletter-signup/

ACKNOWLEDGMENTS

This version of *At Last in Laguna* comes to you seven years after I wrote the original book. When I received my rights back from my former publisher, I was excited to update and edit Alyssa and Brandt's story. I've fixed some technical editing issues, fleshed out some areas, and teased you with a new epilogue.

I wrote this book with Kay Bennett's tireless encouragement, relentless cheerleading, and positive reinforcement. My big brother Robert Petretti—thanks for all of your help, editing advice, and encouragement. Leslie Hachtel—Without your encouragement and excellent advice, this series wouldn't have lifted off of the ground. Thank you so much for your generosity.

Kerrigan Byrne—thanks for your assistance with all things Celtic! And, thank you for your encouragement and advice: you have no idea how much it means to me. You're an inspiration and I'm so happy my fan-girling over you blossomed into a true friendship.

Finally, to Todd for giving me the space to write. I love you. And, finally to my furry kids: Lola, Beau, Josie, and Daisy, thanks for providing me daily laughs and all the cuddles.

ALSO BY CLAIRE MARTI

Pacific Vista Ranch Series

Nobody Else But You

The Very Thought of You

For The Love of You

Wrapped Up with You

The Wonder of You

California Suits Series

Hotel King

Wine Country King

Monterey King

Holiday Queen

Palm Springs King

Romance in Laguna Beach Series

Second Chance in Laguna

At Last in Laguna

Sunset in Laguna

ABOUT THE AUTHOR

Claire Marti is an award winning and *USA Today* Bestselling author of swoonworthy Contemporary Romance novels set in Southern California, including the Pacific Vista Ranch series and spin-off California Suits series. She lives in San Diego with her husband, silly dog, and three clever cats.

Claire started writing stories as soon as she was old enough to pick up pencil and paper. After graduating from the University of Virginia with a BA in English Literature, Claire was sidetracked by other careers, including practicing law, selling software for legal publishers, and managing a non-profit animal rescue for a Hollywood actress.

Finally, Claire followed her heart and now focuses on two of her true passions: writing romance and teaching yoga.